A Man About the House

A Breakthrough Book

University of Missouri Press

A Man About the House

A Novella by Ward Dorrance

ISBN 0-8262-0127-X *Paper*
ISBN 0-8262-0128-8 *Cloth*
Copyright © 1972 by
The Curators of the University of Missouri
Library of Congress Catalog Number 72-79643
Printed and bound in the United States of America
University of Missouri Press, Columbia 65201

For Allen Tate

I

WHAT AMAZED HIM WAS THAT HE HAD let it happen. At sixty he was still so quick on his feet; ordinarily so precise, by nature and by habit. "Yonder" in fact, as his American landlady, Mrs. Lightfoot, would have said was why he had learned the craft of repairing watches.

Moreover, out of the corner of his eye, he had seen the picture move; had even heard the squeal of the nail when it left the plaster. There had been plenty of time to leap up and catch it—the tinted photograph of his parents. And yet there he had sat at his work table, gawking like a steer, while his father, seated, and his mother, standing with a hand upon her husband's shoulder, had slid downward past the roses of the wallpaper and hit the floor in a cloud of dust and powdered glass.

He tried to smile at his concern. No one, no secondhand dealer, would have given him a dime for the thing, either for the print or for its carved frame. Still, something about it had impelled him to carry it all the way from home at the top of his pack. Something had caused him to stitch up a canvas cover to fit it; to protect it from sleet and from drizzle. And there was no good, now, in his pretending that he had simply been startled by the noise of its fall.

He was deeply dismayed by it; pinched, somewhere down within himself; anguished, and he did not have to think of it; he *saw* it; saw it with his own two eyes in his reflection on the face of a clock nailed up against the wall before him.

It was a kitchen clock, hung in a ring of watches yet to be worked on; with a glass wide enough to select him where he sat, the way a telescope could pick up a goat on a mountain ledge. There he was, all of him down to the belt; his chunky blond head; his blue eyes, of a blue all the more grieved because the convex glass made the blue seem to "run." There he was; his square chin; his meaty shoulders; all exact, even to the spitefully clear miniature of his humpback.

He had been born with the hump. He had not been kicked by a horse, or run over. And there had been nothing to do about it. As a matter of fact, as humps went, it was a neat and compact one, not hard for a tailor to cover over. It was simply inconvenient ("ill" convenient, as Mrs. Lightfoot would say again) because it prevented him from turning his chin to the right and quite closing his mouth, and because a left club foot had seemed to come with it. The worst of it perhaps was that the thing appeared to have a modest life of its own; to be in truth a creature apart from him but which he had to carry about, and which sometimes levelled its hairless lids above his shoulder—"promenading the eye" as *Maman* said, she being from a French-speaking canton.

It might be that the clue to his present distress lay in that word, *Maman*.

It surely had little to do with Daddy, who did not count—not in that way, quite. He was huge, German or at any rate Teutonic, breathless, pacific, blue-eyed under a fringe of gold hair (as he was now in the picture on the floor) and mutely surprised at everything, including the fact that people thought him in league with the devil for misbegetting a son. "All as it is and all in good time," he told the boy, whom he called *der kleine Otto*. He was, when Otto thought back over it, a sort of tender hippopotamus.

When you moved from him to *Maman*, you turned a page. She was Gaulish, tiny, with a kinky black head and fast black eyes and hairy bowlegs; spoke German when she had to, as if she'd been spitting out grains of glass; and was wed to the love of her son almost as nuns marry Christ. Random occasions to defend him were not enough. She looked for others.

When he came in from school she was nearly always in the kitchen, an open alcove off the *salle*, the big low-beamed room with a fireplace, where they ate and "lived." There she sweated under a head-cloth, frowning in the heat; dim at first in the light from slits in the firebox of the stove. *Elle faisait au four* naturally—she was baking something for him; and at the sight of him would manage to smile and bow and, with her thumb and forefinger, make the gesture of pulling an odor out of her nose, so as to call his attention to the smell of vanilla or anise. There would be small cakes giving off a good smell in the oven.

"What in class today?" she would call out.

"Algebra and a French theme," he might answer, "then the life of a saint in Latin."

It did not matter much at this point what he

said. She did not know what algebra meant. It and themes too were a lot of stuff for men. At the word "saint," however, she brightened and slammed the oven door as if she had all the saints alive inside the stove. Let them roast until they healed her boy. Sometimes, as she was fond of saying, you had to be rough with them.

She had not yet got to her real interrogation, actually.

While the cakes cooled on a rack; while pots gurgled in the ringed light about the stove lids; while, in short, she had a few moments before Daddy would come kicking the snow from his shoes at the door, she drew Otto down onto the divan in the *salle*, to get at what the Americans call "brass tacks."

At recess had the boys slapped his hump? Did they call it "Monk?" Did they let him play at games with them? . . . Ah, and above all, had he seen the girls? Had he met the crocodile they made on the way to their own school? Were they nice to him?

There was no ducking the shrewd black of her eye or the rattle of her questions. When he tried to protest that after all, he was seventeen now, she sniffed; folded her hands across the wet spot in the middle of her apron, and waited. Usually he was obliged to admit that he had had fair success with the boys, none at all with the girls.

These last, when he had come upon them—blond, pink, plump, already broad in the hip—had been marching in line, singing, switching their green-pleated uniform skirts in unison; moving from one patch of pine trees to another, over the gravel of the road along the cliff above the valley. At the sight of him they hesitated, fell out of step and halted their song. They did not quite know what to do. Each smiled, but as if each had got a thorn in the corner of her mouth. They moved by him (where he stood in the snow to one side in yellowed bracken); they called out, "Good morning, Otto Reinherz"; and, giggling and pushing one another, made for the next group of pines.

"*Oh, quels coeurs de corbeaux!*" *Maman* cried, and made two fists and hoped the girls would catch the mange.

"No, no, no," Otto would say gently. "You know quite well how it is. You know that I shall never have one of those." And he would add, "You do know that—that I shall never have one of them, or a woman of any kind."

Apparently he spoke once too often. One evening, instead of weeping, she rose angrily from the couch, snapping her fingers. "*Ah ça! On verra ce qu'on verra!*," she said, "We'll see about that!"

He watched her uneasily later; while she "ladled out" and when she cleared away and washed up. He trembled to think, but knew he would never guess, what plan she had adopted.

Perhaps he would have to eavesdrop, to find out.

Often at night, when his parents, in the next room of the loft, had left off creaking the springs and being what *Maman* called "hygienic," he listened to their talk. It was frequently of himself. They were afraid lest he not have a normal life; that he would have to remain an unwilling and un-balanced celibate. He shared their dread. So did the boys at school, if you called dread what could be expressed in sniggers and guffaws. The boys at school, with gloating grins for their own hopes, had told him all about that. What they had to shout, and his parents to say under their breath, had bitten in deep. The dipping of his club foot, when he walked, seemed to tap out the rhythm for it . . . . But, at one point, he was on the side of the boys at school: like them he would have suffered any pang on earth rather than have his *mother* push publicly into his life. Particularly if her jostling had anything to do with girls.

He trembled, for two reasons. First, she was not afraid, as she put it, "to say boo to a goose." Sexual intercourse she called "hygiene," and, when there was natural occasion to mention it, made no more of it than she'd make of slipping a bit into a horse's mouth. Second, whenever Otto's fate was in question, she loved battle. She courted it. In a slight difference with the woman next door, she was capable of bringing a hoe handle down across her neighbor's nose, pleasantly biting her own under lip. What might she not, in her ire, do about "the girls," the pretty pink things with swinging skirts? And in his wonder of this sort, he was alone. Daddy did not help. Daddy, once consulted, had only said, "No male mind will ever know what the female mind will do next." That was all. Except that he had shifted his weight to his other hip . . . which was, for him, not easy . . . and sagely added, "If you can call the female mind a mind. It may be something else."

Unfortunately, on the night when Otto had resolved to listen, his room was moonlit, with a humming wind at the window pane. He was tired. The combination of a soft featherbed, the humming and the moon, put him to sleep. He missed the talk, if there had been any.

But at breakfast he was restless and suspicious. His mother *sang*, and banged pans about at the stove. From where he sat at table, waiting with his hands upon the checkered cloth, even the back of her neck looked like the neck of a woman who had taken a decision.

She had. She had done so. But it was not until the next Saturday that he could be sure; that he could even guess which.

Their house, a small wooden one with an overhanging roof, one of a type which English visitors persisted in calling a *shallie*, lay on a slope facing the road at the edge of the cliff above the drop. The land fell away so fast that it had, indeed, three floors, two rooms on each. What would have been the basement still had windows opening upon the pines, and upon a town which suddenly appeared far off, in miniature because of the distance, downward between their trunks; a tiny stone town showing blocks of steep-roofed houses as it might in a woodcut, around a cathedral with spires in a bare *platz*, before a dock on a lake; all between two cliffs—one wooded; one of clean rock with the tail of a waterfall, soundless in its veiled wiggling. Off over that, a range of blue hills.

Maman called this room the *atelier*. It was here that Daddy sat all day repairing clocks and watches and here, on Saturdays, at a long table under a line of timepieces hanging on the wall above, that he taught Otto how to repair and even to make watches. It was an old, father-to-son-to-grandson sort of thing, cobwebby and slow; so nearly motionless from moment to moment that, though they were concerned with Time, one might have thought that that was just what they had no regard for. But there was no nonsense permitted. It was a dawn to nighttime job, with bread and beer and cheese at noon. The seat of Otto's pants often longed to rise, to restore the circulation; but he did not dare; there was Daddy's frown and slow breathing and the danger of putting Daddy off his pitch by a sudden motion.

Hence, on the Saturday after *Maman*'s decision, he was bewildered to see the old man pause and yawn when it only said a quarter to three by all the watches . . . bewildered and baffled out of his wits when the old man added (still in the yawn), "What if we took a stretch to the village? *Si nous allions chez les filles donc?*"

It was the suddenness; the command within the suggestion that they visit a "house," coming from one's own usually tongue-tied dad, that shook Otto; that paralyzed his tongue. Not that the latter mattered. With *Maman* it was possible to discuss, even on occasion to shout; she liked an uproar that raised echoes and brought neighbors to the fence. With Daddy it would not work. He settled every argument, loud or soft, by presenting his blank blue eyes, like those of a bobbing, blown-up balloon figure in the carnival parade; by merely showing his shoulders and, so to speak, his still broader silence.

Otto was out in the sunlit road; stumbling in the gravel somewhat behind (where Daddy would expect to find a woman or a child); making such speed as he could with his club foot, before it even occurred to him to ask questions. By then it was too late. There was nothing to address but the oblong of his father's back, moving only under the torso; the arms limp; the rough shoes, like an enlisted man's, taking the same number of steps per quarter-kilometre. Nothing to talk to but that pacific, settled back; nothing to speak with but down, deep down, his own self—where however, as Mrs. Lightfoot would say, there was a God's plenty to commune with. There was, for instance, as low down as what the boys called his "gonads," a gibbering little freak of a monster all too eager to get up doubts.

The old man had said, "Let us go to a 'house.'" And so, the old one being the old one, with such a tread in the gravel, "To a 'house' we shall go"—so Otto knew. But the monster squeaked, "Ah-ah. And who's going to do what, when we get there? You know in reason it is not going to be your father." (Somehow, every time Otto relived this, and tried to put it into English, as he attempted to get everything, for practice, Mrs. Lightfoot got into the act. Against his better judgment, he took his "English" cue from her.) "No," Otto answered, "it will not be Pa—I mean my father." The monster waited; waited to give greater effect to the clearing of its throat; coughed and said briefly, "He's wore out from home." Otto agreed. "Furthermore," he wished to add, "he's of a nature not to wish to step on a dog's tail . . . ." "Not to step on *no* dog's tail," the thing said primly, and before Otto could comment, it let out the worst:

"Make up your mind. What *are* you going to do when you get there? Stand around sending out postals to the folks back home? Or are you going to face a naked woman your Ma's age? And *you*," there the monster gave a supple trill, "you having somehow or other to git *with* her, or make a damned fool of yourself?"

*　　　*　　　*

Otto fell behind. With a desperate look across the valley at the cathedral in the *platz* (a tiny spider of a carriage was pulling away from the door), he stopped; blamed his pace on his club foot. But once more it was too late. Daddy, hearing silence behind him, called out without turning around, "*Mais va toujours, und mach schnell, que diable!*"

*　　　*　　　*

There was nothing for it but to do as Daddy said; *make speed*—club foot or not. They had already gone down three dips in the road and around two bends, where the pines found more room to grow. Just beyond the first stone houses of the village, they took a street behind the church square; a lane really, but between damp walls so close you could touch them, with a gutter full of soapy water in the middle. It narrowed. The lane narrowed up ahead, toward a faded pink house before which they presently stood. It occupied a diminutive *platz* by itself. A full two-story gallery surrounded it. Mossy baskets of geraniums, hanging from the lower one, dripped water into Otto's neck and made his teeth chatter while Daddy raised echoes with the knocker on the door.

It was answered, not by a slut, picking her teeth, but by a quiet woman who might well have been the portress of a convent—white-haired, with a white coif of some kind. Folding her hands before her, she stood on the top one of three stone steps and took in the scene below.

"What age have you, my son?" she said, blinking her lashes at Otto, but it was Daddy who answered, "Seventeen years *et plus*." He stated it heavily. It made the woman smile. "*Entrez alors; soyez les bienvenus*," she said. With a rounded elbow of welcome she drew them both inside. Otto was gaping at a front hall; a varnished, crooked stairway to the left; a chaste parlor—with chairs around a bench to the right; the whole of it chilly, and, as Mrs. Lightfoot often said of her own hallway, "waxed to a fare-you-well."

The woman was annoyed that Otto had followed in his knock-kneed way into the room behind her and Daddy, who had settled down on the bench and crossed his knees. She began, "But go up, my boy, go upstairs," in the tone of a teacher who would slap your face if a parent were not there . . . but at once admitted, "Pardon, I forgot. Go up. Take Number 202," and gave Otto a shove, sharper than Daddy saw, toward the yellow-varnished stair. He clumped up as far as the landing; paused and looked back. The woman, holding the fingers of one hand pressed over those of the other, was explaining that the Number 202 had the specialty of initiating *les commençants*. "*Entendu, ma soeur*," Daddy said easily. Light shone on his glasses in the late glow from a west window.

There was nothing for Otto to do but go forward . . . on up, on his good foot and on what the boys called his "flipper" . . . on up to where a beam of light spread out on the upper floor, near, as it happened, to Number 202.

He halted and peered inside. No explosion occurred. There was nothing but a rosecolored curtain; a narrow bed with a rather more than plump nude woman lying on top of the sheets. She wore her hair in a blond rope; her doll-baby blue eyes were blank; she was playing with one breast and, until she saw the corner of his hat, hummed a tune. Her stomach mounted into a mound: below it—this was a complete surprise to him—she seemed to be astraddle of something like a muff. Then there were her knees and her toes and she was calling out, "Cut the nonsense, kid! Come on in! It'll all be easy!"

She did not say, "It'll all be fun," and for that he was to think of her afterwards with something like affection. She knew. Very probably she knew that he would never feel limper than when he drew his trousers off, or pimplier-chillier than when he unbuttoned his shirt—both at her curt directions. He turned to her in despair, "Ah," she said, "you don't trust me!" . . . . And she was right. She had little arts. Casual and almost grim little devices for provoking little things; hurrying little things and getting rid of little things. In less time than it took to tell (that was an English idiom) she was leading him, to a wash stand at the foot of the bed where, from a scalloped purplish bowl, she showed him how to clean himself with a wad of cotton and a bit of alcohol.

It was that quick. He would have had almost nothing to remember, one way or the other (except for the bite of the alcohol), had the woman not, at the last moment, when she was throwing the cotton away, asked if she might touch his hump.

"They say it brings luck," she said.

"Go ahead," he said. And she did. He was used to such requests, but had never been affected by them as he was while he pulled on a pant leg and, over one shoulder, watched her examining her finger as if she had picked her nose with it. Why did that hurt? Why did he care if some scrofulous girl (he began to hate the poor woman) thought he was a sort of dwarf? But it did wound him, so that, in the now almost dusky gravel of the road home, when his father asked, "How was it?", he answered bitterly:

"Nothing. It was nothing at all," he said. "Is that all there is to it?"

To his surprise, because when his father asked a question he normally thought he had done enough and did not wait for an answer, his father said distinctly over the rattle of gravel beneath their feet, "No. That is not all there is to it."

The rest was a hoarse strike of six from the cathedral out of a growing fog across the lake; and his mother's snap of a towel (like a waiter's) by way of welcome at the door. Daddy put on his spectacles to read. Not even *Maman* asked questions. Yet all evening both glanced at him occasionally, as one steals looks at a child who has not liked his Christmas present.

*   *   *

How odd that all of this could float back up at him out of the dust; out of the dust above the fallen picture, which still lay wrecked on the linoleum of Mrs. Lightfoot's extra chamber! Or rather, how strange that all of this—these odors, actions and situations—did not drift back as "memories," but remained smartly present, "as smart as cat dung" as Daddy would say; far from past; still to be lived through. They were not subjects of a half-pleasant nostalgia, recollections of boyhood in Switzerland, pressed edelweiss in an album of verses and all that; and not a ground for what the Americans called "a spell of the blues." He would only go so far as to take a clue from the Americans. He called it "thinking blue." What he meant, quite, he did not know. He was only certain that, when the thing came on (as it had when the picture fell), it was as it was at times when he'd all but stepped upon a snake, a serpent with its hissing mouth drawn back over the flat of its coil, and himself with one foot still in the air.

Snakes; that sounded theatrical; sometimes, to be sure, the snake was a small one; not enough to make all that fuss over. Indeed, what vexed him was not snakes but definitions, diagnoses. As a watchmaker, he was not accustomed to leave them ragged. What did he mean . . . *precisely* . . . by "thinking blue?" It had to do (this little he was sure of) with having to live in the past and the present at the same time; but wasn't that dangerous for a chronologist supposedly in his right mind? . . . Did it happen to other people? He had never had the wit . . . or the courage . . . to ask. He did not actually know it to be true of any living man, but he could think of one dead one; a man named (speaking of hair-raising snakes) Saint Augustine of Hippo.

In his school days, in the one room of small desks and one big desk around a stove, he and the older boys in advanced Latin had been set to translating excerpts from the works of holy men, notably the *Confessions* of Augustine. In those times, of course, the text had been chiefly gibberish; a matter of patching up fat words like *abundantia* with verbs of which the original suggested nothing in French or German. And yet something, a little, had apparently rubbed off. He had retained the impression that the saint believed that Time did not die but continued alive on into the present. And he himself believed it.

How could he fail to believe it? Here he was on his chair before his table in Mrs. Lightfoot's chamber, walling his eyes about as if for help from his army cot, under its shelf of mechanic's manuals; from his one north window where a breeze held out the pink curtain which Mrs. Lightfoot thought "went so well" with the scarlet roses in the wallpaper. And here he was beside *Maman* on the goat hide couch at home. And yet here he saw the curtain stir; heard Mrs. Lightfoot arguing with Mrs. Courtright, the landlady next door, down below in the yard beneath the window. For a moment it was touch and go (an English idiom) to know which would claim his attention.

Maman won out.

It was on the evening of the day which Otto, sometimes fearfully, sometimes wistfully, called "the day of the 'house.'" As clearly as he saw Mrs. Lightfoot's waxed linoleum at his feet, he smelled *Maman's* wiry curls and felt her loose breastiness as she pulled him down beside her. The divan was long, with a tasselled antimacassar of her knitting. His feet were among the cats and the one great dog before a fire, which lay now in orange-and-blue-colored coals, tinkling between the high andirons. In that heat she meant to have the truth.

"It did not work, eh?" she asked. She did not beat about the bush; as Otto had once protested, she did not know where any bush was.

He took a moment to answer; a moment to note that he had been right; that the plan of the visit to the "house" had been hers; and shrugged his shoulders as well as he could in her grasp. She had put her arms around him; knotted her hands over the bony seam of his hump; she was looking him in the eye. "*Oui et non*," he said.

She let him go. "You need not play–act with me," she said. "I am broad–minded . . . . Was she nice to you at least?"

Otto shrugged again. "She did what was needed no doubt," he said, and stared to see her close her eyes as if they ached and open them wildly and hear her hoarsely whisper. "*Oh mon petit*, have patience. Wait. Some day you will find one that will be only yours." At that she wept; kissed him repeatedly full on the mouth; and said again, in a kind of fury, "You wait! That woman will love you *because* of your hump!"

*   *   *

This scene had exhausted her apparently. For some days she was silent and saggy, not remembering where she had left certain pots in her kitchen. In the end it took a neighbor to revive her; to sound the trump. They—she and Otto—were "out in front," gathering pine cones for kindling. *Maman*, wandering off alone, approached the fence. Presently she was talking with *la voisine*. Most probably the latter, a bald and harmless, freckled woman with a shawl over her head, had ventured to say that Otto and his father had been seen to enter the *maison close*, *chez la Mère Céleste*. Indeed it was something like that, and *Maman* seemed to take it as a relieving signal. Her back went straight; she clutched the fence with both hands; her head bobbed like a mechanical toy's; she let out the air in her lungs in at least two statements that Otto got entire. One was a rapid order: "Go milk your cow and drink the blue milk, you poor sow!" The second, in a scream, crushed the neighbor still more. "My son will have a normal life, do you HEAR? Do you HEAR? Pick out your ears! He will have a normal life, do you HEAR? If I have to go to bed with him myself!"

*　　*　　*

That had settled the neighbor and Otto as well. He had never forgot it. It would have come back full, in any country where he heard the wind and smelled pine cones and heard the sound of milk in a pail . . . but to tell the truth the women, also, of all countries goaded him on a bit; helped him on a bit with the theories of Saint Augustine by their frequent doing of business over fences.

They were at it now . . . down below the pink curtain, Mrs. Lightfoot, his landlady, and Mrs. Courtright, her opposite number across the way. It was the increasing shrillness of their voices that attracted his attention. He did not have to look down to see them. Mrs. Courtright was a short, fleshy person with large-flowered dresses and a spayed fox terrier bitch. Mrs. Lightfoot wore a cap threaded by a ribbon, the hem of which lay over her greying blond wisps and her popped, oyster-colored eyes. At the end of her long legs, her "bunny rabbit" slippers slid along in the dust when she "did" his room with her push mop. He hated dust, on principle, and because it was a danger to his opened watches. She loved raising it, as a sign of good housewifery; she was fond of repeating, "If we ever split, Mr. Otto Reinherz, it'll be over dust."

The two women were standing, he knew, one to either side of a stake-and-rider fence grown with convolvulus *Pearly Gate* and *Heavenly Blue*; each holding a mop; each thrusting her chin into the leaves and talking thirteen to a dozen. Normally he did not listen: a typical exchange would go:

"What are you doing today?"

"I'm baking today."

"Oh, you're baking today."

"Yeah, I'm baking today."

But this morning, he thought they were speaking of him, and, with a faint smile, he did prick up his ears. Sure enough, while he sat still, Mrs. Courtright distinctly said that she'd heard deformed men were worse after women than the normal ones.

This brought a snort. "You talk like being after women was bad in the first place." That was Mrs. Lightfoot's voice. It had a natural bleat, but she had tried to make it firm.

"Just the same," Mrs. Courtright said—of the two she had the deeper chest tones—"Just the same, I wouldn't take his money."

"You'd take anything you could git from a stout gentleman under seventy." That was Mrs. Lightfoot again, but Mrs. Courtright, only interrupted, was going on:

"I run a clean house, myself—ouch!" she said, "you hurt!"

Apparently she had caught a blow from Mrs. Lightfoot's mop handle, but she sucked her knuckle and went on. "You know he spends every weekend at Lola Henderson's," she said, "and you know what she is."

Mrs. Lightfoot had thought of something better, not perhaps distinguished in the line of logic, but pleasurable. "What," she asked, "about you and that Mr. Harbaugh that had your tower room?"

"Years ago." Mrs. Courtright wiped that one away.

"*Two* years ago," Mrs. Lightfoot said. "Not long enough to excuse no little girlish skedaddle. You cried and cried when he taken the train."

"As I say"—Mrs. Courtright got back to the subject levelly—"your Mr. Heartburn or whatever he calls hisself (Otto Somebody) spends every weekend with Lola Henderson, the chief whore in town, as sure as God made apples and you know it and you go into his room with him and take his money. I wouldn't. I run a clean house, myself."

There were sounds of a skirmish. "If that mop comes up alongside my head again," Mrs. Courtright said, "I'll pull up the fence. You won't be around here for a while."

*   *   *

Otto let their voices fade out; heard only the anger in them; for him it was a re-enactment; above their squabble he heard his mother's voice (for volume she'd have had the prize); heard her scream, "My boy will have his life if I have to get in with him"; the day she was having her own bit over the fence—she and the poor drab with the shawl and the cow.

It was, so far as he could tell, literally *du déjà vu.* The two women were there; mother with a basket of pine cones, the neighbor with a wooden pail for milk. There was no nonsense about "remembering" them. Or of recalling that it was because of his deformity that *Maman* was yelling obscenities. There was no need to rebuild the past scene. The two women were there *now;* eye to eye over the paling *now*. He saw his mother's lifted fist and the neighbor's half-witted gape under her shawl, even smelled their smoky country-women's dresses, *now*. The two were as present to him while he sat there in his chair as were Mrs. Lightfoot and Mrs. Courtright, fencing with mops below, amidst the morning glories.

In the end it was the *nowness* of the thing that shook him, more than the quarrel or the cause of the quarrel—his own disgusting body. It was the overlapping of the past across the official present that made him look up, wide-eyed, at the clock on the wall before him, as if lightning, out of a clear sky, had cleft a tree close at hand.

He sat for a while, uneasy. Mrs. Lightfoot had finished outside. She was at the sink, doing her breakfast dishes, on the floor below. Over the rush of tap water she was singing, "*O, may no earthly cloud arise!*" To the tune of that, his mind drifted. For a moment he did not know why he recalled the agitation of an old man back home; a deaf man; a man who, as they said, could not hear thunder. Standing at his window one day he went into hysterics (during a gale that made no sound for him) to see the wind uproot an ancient pear tree just at his nose beyond the pane. For weeks he went about the village pulling at people's sleeves, trying to persuade them of what they knew—that the tree; *a* tree; a *whole* tree had come out of the earth and stood erect, upright a moment, madly shaking its fruit, before it lay out on the ground in a soft, silent crash. Even calmed and brought out of his fit, the old chap spilled his beer in wonder. In what called itself the natural world he had, as plain as he had eyes, taken in something unnatural. And nobody would try to understand.

Now, after some forty years, Otto did get the point. He had only to look down at the floor of his room; at the photograph under its powdered and slivered glass. His father had no features; his face had been shaved off. His mother's smiling head, in its best hat, lay off aside, a little to the left of its shoulders.

It was all well enough to argue that a wind can bring a pear tree down, and that nails holding pictures may come loose. There *was*, after all, a shudder; a physically crawly feel of outrage in such happenings; more for Otto than for the old man perhaps, because, for Otto, the happenings always brought on a tightening sense of the oneness of Time.

What of that, or what ought there to be of that? What was so wonderful about it, if it had been known since the days of Saint Augustine, maybe centuries before him? Especially why, when the truth of it came over Otto (as it was coming now) need he feel it as menacing; as swollen with ill?

No doubt the answer lay in the shake of the old man's pear tree. It simply seemed to violate the common sense of right-minded shopkeepers—dancing trees, beheaded mothers; what man who sold beef, what little woman who dealt in thread and thimbles, would halt long over such as that?

And yet, and yet, and yet the answer (if there was one) could not be trumped up like that. The answer was never simple. It was, if you liked, of a mortuary green with a whiff of mould about it. And it always, with no trace of reason, brought on something nasty. And something impossible to untangle; something with its saxifrage hair roots deep in rock.

Why now when he saw his mother's face, for instance, should a brutal peasant proverb flood his brain? In French it went: "*Là où le nombril est enterré, faut bien que la chèvre y broûte?*" He even fingered it about in English, and could make of it only: "*Where the nanny goat's navel string is buried, there must her kid do its grazing.*"

Nothing much there. Nothing except the chill between his mother's grave in Switzerland and the chair on which he sat in this room above the Missouri River.

Apparently one did not look upon pear trees in their travail without peril. Presently—he missed the tool he had been reaching for and dropped the tiny spring of a watch on the floor—he gave up. Presently, precisely because it was ghostly nonsense, he knew that he had to see Lola Henderson at once. And with a hand on one hip he hobbled out of the room, fast and sidewise, as Mrs. Lightfoot would say, "like a tromped on spider."

II

BY THAT TIME, MRS. LIGHTFOOT HAD
reached the front hall in her cleaning; tall under her
headrag, clicking her mop against the baseboards.
At the sight of his taking the stairs two at a time,
which would have been fast for a man with both
good feet, her jaw dropped. Seeing him hobble towards her, his face red and distorted, she pulled out
the hall table; got behind it and said, "Don't you
lay a finger on me! Not *here* you don't!"

But he had sped by her, and hope faded from her
pink-rimmed eyes. The most she could do (now
that she divined his errand) was to quaver at his
back, "This here's a Thursday. I taken Friday to
be your day!"

Even that he barely heard. He was out on the
sidewalk, dazedly looking over at the chicory weed
which bloomed blue at the rim of the cliff; at the
crumbling bluff top across the street; at the broad
river in its bend below it. He was still confused;
ashamed of his flight; not daring yet to probe into
its cause.

"Let us think of something else," he said. "Let
us think that I probably stopped here to live because
of that drop down to the river."

But that was a mistake. Immediately there
popped into his mind that other drop; the one down
to the lake at home, near the spot where his people
lay buried.

To check himself, he wheeled about to stare at

the houses of "the ladies," as he called Mrs. Court-right and Mrs. Lightfoot.

None but theirs in the block—the two left end ones—had remained "homes"; others had been taken over by cobblers, cleaners and dyers, and undertakers. All were alike, or nearly, two-story castle-like structures with grey stone fronts; brick sidewalls; Gothic turrets that served no purpose; balconies too narrow to sit on—"mighty classy pieces of property" as the ladies described them.

"And that," he said, "ought to do me."

He limped on away from Mrs. Lightfoot's, past Mrs. Courtright's on the corner. The latter had screened in her porch and installed a swing, in which she now sat with her panting terrier beside her. She said quietly, seeing Otto pass, that she would swan. "Him going to Lola Henderson's in the middle of the week," she added, more clearly, to be sure he heard, "and him with that built-up shoe."

He kept his eyes down and did not answer. He had turned the corner. He was now in Monroe Street, a street which descended at first so steeply that it could have done with stairs; which then crossed what must once have been a creek bed; and mounted thereafter to the High Street, again on such a grade that steps would have been a help. But it was lined solid with shops—of Jewish clothiers beckoning him in; Negroes laughing outside their barbecue pits; and German butchers with banana-like clusters of knockwurst in the windows. Otto loved it. He could be comfortably lost in it. The Jews were almost humpbacked themselves; the

Negroes did not care whether a poor man had two shoulders or three; and the Germans, unloading a pig or a haunch of veal, were also jolly.

And now here it all was, just as it had been on his first trip out into town from Mrs. Lightfoot's house; when he'd arrived, a wanderer in a strange country; the evening when he had met the sailor; the evening when the sailor had taken him to Lola's.

How funny the sailor had looked! Not sober of course; small; but tidy, neatly dressed in blues, with a white cap atop his black forelock and his black eyes. What an odd sight in that seedy, land-bound, hilly street . . . . And when he spoke, how mysterious! Cocking an eye up at Otto, he had asked, "Was you by chancest out looking for any, mister?"

Otto, not understanding, shook his head, think-ing that the easiest way out. But he did hope the sailor would not pass on and leave him alone in the crowd. The sailor was undersized and knotty, like a Bantam rooster; he was droll, he made company; his uniform was calming, something official in a hoarse and jostling throng. Therefore when he asked if Otto did not at least wish to walk about and see the town, Otto nodded vigorously. He had got that bit. And off they set together, Otto keeping up by hobbling two steps to the sailor's most unsteady one.

The High Street, when they had finally climbed up to it, looked grand. It stretched out along a straight ridge, loftier, really, than the ladies' houses at the bluff edge over the river. Globes of light were beginning to come on in the dusk, above the street's smoothly gravelled width. At one end of it a state capitol, a kind of domed Roman temple, rose up in a park. At the other stood a penitentiary, a fortress bristling with keeps and crenellations. In between, the showcases of elegant shops were now brilliantly lit. Otto especially remembered Dallmeyer's Department Store, where they stopped to rest—Otto to watch the few carriages still passing by, with here and there a motorized taxi, chuffing on like a toy that might stop at a chair leg; the sailor to explain that he was just in this place on leave for a few days to visit an aunt and God knew why. She could not cook and spent most of her time in church.

Here Otto, seeing that his friend was cross (and perhaps sobering up too fast), broke in to suggest that perhaps they might stop in somewhere nearby to have a beer.

"Haw! I already got me one of them," the sailor said and laughed, revived by his own joke. "But you sure hit the nail on the head," he added. "We'll go wet our whistles. But not no beer, eh? We're going to ask for two double Bourbons. Got that straight?"

"Good, agreed," Otto cried, to have something to say. Once more he had not understood. But when he had followed through the louvered doors of a bar in the track of the sailor, he stood abashed. Before him stretched a room long enough that it seemed to have an artificially drawn perspective; with a low roof; a flat cloud of cigar smoke descending almost to the heads of a line of elderly men in broadcloth, with heavy watch chains, men whose bald heads and limp chaps were doubled amidst the misty twinkles of a mirror across the bar before them.

"This is not for us," Otto whispered. And sure enough, behind the crook of the bar, the part nearest the door, bare for the moment of customers, there stood beckoning a heavy blond German whose ears and one-sided nose suggested the prize ring. He was calling, just so as to be heard, "Hey Mac!" to the sailor.

Otto reached them soon enough to hear the man's deep hiss:

"You ain't blind; you know this is the Madison House. You know these tubs behind you is all senators and whatnot. You know damned well I can't sell to no gobs in here, and," he added with a look at Otto's blue denim shirt and old canvas suit, "not no workmen."

"Screw you," the sailor said. He made a fist—harmlessly; his arm was too short, the bar too broad. The German looked bored. It was Otto who stopped what was about to be a scene.

He smiled and pulled the boy back; took his place, and said, "*Bitte, Herr Hauptmann*, if you please, sir," and he could afford to smile again because the German almost did. Relaxed lines appeared about his eyes. He was not a *Herr* anything, but he did not mind being called so. Otto followed closely. "*Herr Hauptmann*," he was careful to repeat, "you see this young man's state. He may cause a scandal. Will you not please be so kind as to give us one drink? I will take him to the back wall. We will drink fast and quietly. We will soon be gone."

The barkeeper hesitated. He examined Otto's eyes; took in the crooked neck, the hump; shrugged his shoulders; reached for two polished glasses and said, "Okay, okay, then. One drink and it's out wid the two of you."

The sailor had pushed around Otto. He leaned over the bar. "One drink!" he crowed angrily. "One for each man, that the way it is? Then make 'em triples, triples on the rocks and lean on it baby! You hear? Or you ain't going to find a bouncer that can run me down. I'll git in between them senators' lags."

The bartender looked, not at the sailor but at Otto, with a patient smile; handed over the triples; took Otto's pay and tip; and said, as if they had been alone, "Stuff something in his mouth. Get him out of here fast."

"Up yours," the sailor cried. But he allowed himself to be led to the wall swiftly, not, as Otto was soon to find, because he had been subdued, but because he had made more interesting plans. Once in safety and in quiet, he swallowed his own drink; accepted half of Otto's; looked out over the dark-clad crowd; advised whoever wished to listen that he had never been able to stand a crowd of *men* all bunched up, and added that he could tell there wasn't going to be anything doing in here. To Otto personally he said, much too loudly, "Back yonder where I run into you and ast you if you was out cruisin' for some, you said no. Have you by any chancest changed your mind?"

This time, aided by the whiskey and the boy's leer, Otto caught on. He wiped his mouth; calculated that he had not been hygienic for over a month; remembered that he had promised to leave soon anyway; and peered down into the youngster's eyes. "Yes," he said. "I've changed my mind. Let's go."

The boy grinned. "I knowed all along that you was a sport," he said. "Call me Rob, will you?"

They were out in the street. Rob had tripped up over a fireplug but refused help. He was looking about for his starched cap; found it in the gutter; and rose without stopping talking. "Trust little Robbie," he was saying. "I can smoke it out wherever it's at. Manila, Bangkok, Cairo; you name it. Let alone in a little one-horse town."

Back in the High Street, they passed Dallmeyer's again and the Broken Dollar Store; passed the town hall and its fire brigade on the ground floor. After one, perhaps two, of the darker blocks of houses on beyond, Rob suddenly said, "Jackson. A guy told me it was Jackson," and turned to the right.

Jackson was another down-hill-up-hill street, difficult for Otto at Robbie's pace, but not so dark as he had feared. Away from the lights of High Street there was a moon, bright enough to cast long shadows. He was beside Rob when Rob stopped at a gate and said, "This must be it. Lola Henderson's place."

"How do you know?" Otto asked.

"Because," Rob said simply, "it ain't like the places around it."

So it was not. It stood end-on to the street before a walnut grove; it was wooden, unpainted, its ridge-pole sagged between its two brick chimneys. Its grounds were so large, and the nearest houses (of stone, facing the street) so prim and new that, Otto judged, it must have been a farmhouse, of which the owner had "sold off a piece" now and then as the town needed land. It had become, literally, among its neighbors, a *maison de tolération*.

"What if you went in first?" Otto suggested. He wanted a while to be alone, to take—to digest, so to speak—his bearings, and was pleased when Rob said, "Right!", pulled open the gate and started down the path inside. For a moment he furnished a useful point of reference. By the movement of his shoulders in the moonlight, Otto made certain that the path lay between hedges of a shrub called "Kiss Me at the Gate"; that it turned sharply toward a set of steps; that they and the broad front door looked deserted. Once more the word "farmhouse" came to mind. He felt he knew the type. From his rambles he called it the Kentucky-Tennessee-Missouri house; brick, with two windows to either side of a door, "chimbleys" at either end and a place for hens to cluck about under the front steps. And he felt as he often had, on the road with his pack, that, if he could ever find a real *heimat* in America, it would be such a place.

Once inside—his knock, like Rob's, had not been answered—the impression fell away. He was not in the front hall of a farmhouse; with a fan tucked behind a calendar, a sepia view of Niagara and another of Grandfather. He stood, rather, in a sort of square reception room, lit from the top by a blueish bulb in a pierced metal shade. It dropped a flickering mauve-colored light over a large table to his right; over a rug which covered the table; over the foot-high statuette which it bore—a cross-legged deity of some kind, sending up a sweet smoke from a hole in the top of its head. To one side a chair, high-backed, with mother-of-pearl designs, almost hid a door which seemed to lead to the hinder parts of the house.

He remained for a while half sitting upon the table; suddenly conscious of his hump and his limp, wishing that he had gone on in company with Robbie into the next room.

It was long, high, furnished by two rows of round tables, each with a beaded pink silk lamp casting its glow over a girl seated beside it—all of them markedly different. They were fat, slim, tall, short, blond, red-headed, dark (one of them a Negress) and all looked bored. One languidly turned the pages of a magazine; another was filing her nails; another flicking her white kid shoes with a handkerchief; still another pumping the treads of a pianola which took up most of the room's far end, all of it except for a staircase leading, with worn treads, to the second floor. They were listening to:

> *"Put your arms around me, baby!*
> *Hold me tight!"*

It was almost time for "the gentlemen" (an occasional sailor did not count). They were "artistes" in the vaudeville about to "go on."

Otto watched them from his shelter, meaning perhaps to remain there; beating time, or thinking time, to the music (so like that of a calliope at a fair); when he, all at once, felt the warmth of a woman close to his left side. It had to be a woman. She was so soft.

For a second, he dared not look around. She had no doubt come in from the back parts of the house, through the door behind the inlaid chair. And she was no doubt the cook. Even over the bite of the deity's incense, she smelled of hickory wood; of kerosene lamps; of kindling and milk and of dough, the floured dough of bread and of cakes scented with anise and vanilla.

She was also short—he saw that much finally by twisting his head about—with a greying pompadour over eyes that were wide, heavily lashed and probably blue. Furthermore she was plump, like a stack of three apples as he had heard said. She had, in any event, plenty to sit upon the table with, beside him; and had a bosom, above her crossed arms, which would have caused *Maman* to exclaim, "*Oh là, là, quelle paire!*"

It prepared him for her voice, which was low and resonant for a woman's when at last she spoke.

"I'm Lola Henderson," she said, with a swallow, a kind of dollop of rural embarrassment in her throat. "I reckon you'd call me the head gramma around here. Fact is, I run this place."

Otto could think of nothing better than to salute her with an "Ah!" and a bow, which in turn caused her to say, "Stranger of some kind, ain't you?", but as if she did not blame him a bit. Indeed she was— and he felt it as if she'd been using her hands upon him—taking in his hump, the angle of his jaw, the turn of his foot. Yet it was still kindly and softly, almost bashfully that she said, "Was you looking for a little companionship?"

"Yes," Otto said. He got it out roundly, feeling that that was only fair. They rose. He took her arm, which she offered, like a nurse, like a parent.

In the pink-lighted room full of bead fringe and wobbly lamps and girls, she began introductions; stopping at one chair; skipping two; halting before another; murmuring as she went, "This here is Cora—make it pretty now, Cora. This is Sue. This is Utah—the girls call her Utah-the-Heater, I don't know why. This is Lulu the colored girl—she's kept especial for Mr. Blitzstein; he runs a print shop over by the capitol? . . . This is Milly—look up, Milly. And this little one we call Effie-the-Wink."

Otto placed his hand on the knee of the last one—thus to settle the matter quickly, but also because Effie, buxom, with yellow rope hair and a doll's marble eyes, reminded him of girls he had come across in such places at home.

And as it happened afterward, she was pleasing. She earned her name; was not repelled by his deformity ("Every gentleman's got *some*thing wrong with him" as she put it); she was, far from eager to get rid of him, inclined to lie a while and chat; to babble disconnectedly like a child, with a little girl's kind of lisping spite. Utah, she confided, for instance, kept a revolver under her handkerchiefs, and not one of those little pearl-handled things, either: Susan would roll a gentleman who had drunk too much, though she denied it: Mr. Blitzstein and Lulu were suspected of getting up some funny tricks together: and old Ma Henderson, as they called her, was fifty-five if she was a day and wasn't even from a town—just from down in the hills. The Ozarks, Effie thought the hills were called. From up in on a creek somewhere. You couldn't trace that.

Otto, listening from his pillow; listening and smiling at the doll-baby, grew sober at the mention of Lola. He had not realized, until he heard her slighted, how much he had felt the warmth of her hip against his on the table; how his heart had gone to meet the charity of her voice; how above all she had instantly not seemed to belong to such a place but to some other that smelled of twirling smoke and dough and spices.

He went back to the house on Friday nights . . . the way, so to speak, having been opened. Went back to Effie. The routine was easier. She appeared to expect it. She thought of him as hers; seemed to have taken him over; indeed, on a night here and there, a Friday night, she would already be upstairs, waiting, in her room.

That was all very well, lucky for a fellow with a hump, or it was not all very well. Not, really. Lying besides the hempen hair and the marble blue eyes, listening to the too-local gossip, it was Lola's hip he kept thinking about—its warmth beside his on the table—as if there had been nothing to her but a warm hip. But there was more; more to think about. She was plump and kind and warm, and what had he, at sixty, to say about a woman's being fifty-five . . . make it fifty, allowing for spite . . . when she had stayed plump and shapely? When she was so good natured and kind (*that* word kept coming back)? When she was so clean as to smell of anise and good brown soap and a scorched ironing board?

Why not admit that she attracted him, not casually, but in the way the magnet on his work table pulled to itself the small screws he used in watches.

Why not confront her and tell her that, childishly, and see what she made of it?

He turned it over in his mind all season, while the leaves turned and ice began to form in the river. One night, which everyone else remembered too, because it brought the first deep cold and froze the river straight across, he met Lola coming down the stairs as he was about to go up. They halted, face to face, beside the pianola. He was breathless, and glad of it. Panting, he could say, like a child asking if she'd like to see his pocket knife, "Why may I not come with you tonight?"

She laughed and he was pleased that she took it that way, pretending to pretend that she did not know at first what he meant. It excused his limp. It made him a boy. A boy blinking under her gaze while she took him and his pocket knife in and laughed again, and after a moment said:

"Pshaw! I give up this business years ago. It kilt my feet, running up and down these here stairs."

She smiled and would have ducked by him, but he moved as she moved, placing his chest against her bosom. He did have *that*, at least, he thought— his great, crippled-man's over-developed chest and shoulders; his ape-like arms and massive thighs. These might incline a really female woman to forgive his hump.

It seemed to do so this time. Lola had stopped trying to get by. She was patting the top of her forward-looped pompadour, gazing up at him with her oddly colored eyes . . . thinking it over . . . speculating . . . weighing the matter, but apparently in his favor at the end, because, still laughing, she said, "But after all, if we went to my place, we'd not have to go up any stairs, would we? My place is down here on the ground floor!" And, exaggerating the grace of her gesture a bit, she took the arm he offered . . . . They traversed the long room, neither noticing that the little Negress was pumping "*You Know You Belong to Somebody Else*" out of the piano; both forgot that Effie-the-Wink lay upstairs, drowsily waiting.

Otto was taken up at once with what he found on the other side of the door, behind the reception room, beyond the violet-lighted hall. Here there were no thick rugs; no heathen gods; not any sweetish incense. Even the pianola sounded far away. He stood in a large, square room, low, with beams made of a tree each. On the left hand, a round table with four chairs crowded a wooden ice chest. On the right, a huge black stove shared the wall with a fireplace, a hearth with polished irons and the coals of a fire. Straight ahead, neatly made with several feather mattresses, the foot of a bed appeared through a door. The whole was lighted by a kerosene lamp, swung from one of the beams above his head.

He stopped, open-mouthed, with both hands making the motion of a man who is feeling of a gossamer or of a spider web. "This is like a cave," he said. "Are there gnomes in here?"

Lola was tying apron strings in the small of her back, watching him with her head to one side. "Gnomes?" she asked. "What's a gnome? We don't even have mice." And she went on, "Are you a Dutchman of some kind? Seem like you can't talk good." And she continued, "This here is just the kitchen ell of an old home place—or was whenever it *was* a home place. My room, there where you see the bed, was a lean-to for wood, tacked on, like. By the way," she added, "it's got an outside door. You can get from there through the garden patch to the privies. Gents' is to the right."

She spoke of privies frankly, but as she'd mention a poker or an ash bucket. They were already friends. Furthermore, she had something else on her mind.

"I expect you could do with a bite," she said. "You'll find light bread in the box—that tin thing on top of the ice chest—maybe some cornbread too —and some buttermilk down below. You get that while I reach down the chicken from the warming oven."

*   *   *

Hours later they were still in rocking chairs to either side of the hearth. A wisp of smoke rose from the blue coals. Each held a sleeping cat in his lap, Lola's a tortoiseshell, Otto's a grey with one white ear, a female that drooled a wet spot on his leg. Otto was saying, evidently not for the first time (Lola was yawning) how like home this was—the hot, crinkling coals; the fragrant fumes; the limp cats; the freedom one dared feel to doze in the puffing lamplight and the shifting shadows.

"*Doze*," Lola said, "*doze*," and added, "that was the mainest word you said. What say we hit the sack, as your sailor boy would put it?"

And they went to bed, undressed by such of the dying firelight as reached the side of the feather bed; not especially interested in one another's nakedness (any more than in the andirons or the cats); each hanging his clothes on hooks, carefully, as if this had been only the latest of years of such nights. Such winter nights. Sleet bit at the window glass. One of the cats tried to get in between them. They slept soundly, like the young, so that at dawn Otto wondered why he had thought it was sleet he had heard popping. The sleet had stopped. There was a light whirl of snow in the air. What he heard was ham in a skillet. Lola had risen and dressed. She was putting eggshells into the coffee, to carry down the grounds.

It was noon before he got back to Mrs. Lightfoot's.

He never saw Robbie, the sailor, again.

III

OH, BUT TODAY HE COULD HAVE USED
a Robbie!

Today when the picture had fallen; when he had
"thought blue"; when he had scuttled out of Mrs.
Lightfoot's house like a frightened child. After all
of that, he'd have welcomed a Robbie's "sass"; his
ruffle and strut; his "Screw you!" to all that vexed
him.

Otto was far from feeling such assurance.

He had escaped Mrs. Lightfoot and turned Mrs.
Courtright's corner. He was on the slope of Monroe
Street again. Down ahead, between the rows of
shops, he heard the same jostling and laughter and
bawling of goods. The same Jews pretended to en-
tice him. The same Negroes said, "How do? How
do?" The same jolly butchers grunted a "*Wie
geht's*?" and touched his hump for luck. One of
them, unloading a van, took out an ox tongue and
waggled it about before his fly. At other times Otto
might have smiled as he smiled at the rest of the
street's happy dirt. Today he glanced aside. He was
not offended, not really. It simply jarred upon him,
as it might have done had he been, say, a mourner
on his way to the graveyard, and if he had seen an
old woman hanging out clothes, a man hoeing
beans, or kids playing marbles. How could others
act as if it were only nine of the clock in the common
sun of another day; how could they reach for ox
tongues or clothespins when he, Otto, was still
"thinking blue?"

It was the same when he had climbed up the far slope of Monroe and reached the High Street. There he stopped for breath as he always did, before the windows of Dallmeyer's Store. This time he frowned to see that one of the displays showed a bride; a blond girl with stone-blue eyes and yellow horsehair lashes, tilted toward a groom in black, with china dentures and a sort of Japanese, chopped-off hair. Thus people not only waggled tongues and hoed beans; they showed you holy matrimony itself as if it were a casual outing. Thus people acted as if the word "normal" need necessarily have any meaning.

Certainly the lady who went by behind him with a sunshade and two little dogs (moving shadows on the window glass) saw nothing odd about the day. Neither did the gentleman who came after her, with a cocked derby and a solid watch chain. Much less did the Negro shouldering a bag of corn. They all knew where they were going.

And thus once more Otto wished for a Robbie; a Robbie who would growl, "What's this stuff about your Momma's grave? We supposed to sit on old folks' coffins? What's this monkey talk about you and 'the dark powers'? Man, you'd turn white if you seen a candle in a punkin."

It would have helped to shake him loose; to let him see the lady with her romping dogs, and the Negro with his corn, as ordinary. Unfortunately there were no sailors about. He stood alone, with his back to the bridal party now; but, at the thought of where he was going, he almost grinned.

He had suddenly recalled another man back home; a blind man, this one, a "dark man" as the old people called him, one who tied a rope from the rear of the house out to the privy, so that he would not have to whimper and dally about for a guide. Just so he himself, figuratively, had fixed a line from Dallmeyer's window to Lola's back door, the one in the ell which led to the kitchen. He had known all along where he was headed. He had no need to say it. The blood in his ears pounded it out. "One more step. Twelve more steps. If I can only get to Lola it will be all right."

But now, moving down High Street, now on the good foot now on the bad, making for the turn-off at Jackson, he thought about Lola and not of himself. What would she say when she opened the door? What could you expect from a woman who suddenly learns that a club-footed man without a change of shirts has come to stay? Would she put an eye to a crack? Would she say, "Well no, now, I don't take people in regular?" . . . What if she said, "Move on. Get out?" His flesh would not carry him back to Mrs. Lightfoot's. His flesh crept to think of the nail hole where the picture had hung.

As matters fell out, Lola did not open the door even a crack. Not at first. She was, as he later realized, at the stove, over a skillet. She had taken his knock for that of a farmer with something to sell. "What say? What say?" she had kept crying, until he had called out his name.

At that, he heard quick soft steps, and the door fell back. Lola filled it. Not the groomed Lola of nights, when she appeared in the hall with leather shoes and a starched dress. What he saw was a short uncorseted woman in a headrag from which curls dropped about her ears; wearing a blue-and-white checkered apron (wet where she had leaned against the sink) and black felt slippers with rosettes like sets of pen wipers.

He spoke to her own straight blue gaze. He begged her pardon. If he might come in, he could explain his appearing at this hour. "No trouble at all," she said, and smiled. "I can stretch this chicken over two people. Come in! Come in!" But her eyes were on his, with a virtuous-suspicious glint. Why had her boy been sent home from school? For shooting paper wads? Dipping a girl's braids in ink? Nobody understood her boy. It was for throwing erasers, she shouldn't wonder.

Meanwhile she drew the door back full. Her voice was warm and glad. Her small, plump hands, when she shook hands with him, were also warm and glad—warm and, so he thought almost in tears as he entered the kitchen, *knowledgeable*; just right for giving an egg one sharp crack, or adding a speck of vanilla. Her touch, as she seemed from her smile to mean it to do, shot a good feeling up his arm. Nothing was wrong. Now that he was here, everything was going to be all right.

You had to hand it to them—to the women. He sat heavily down on a chair by the dining table near the door and handed it to them. Watching her contrive to smile and to frown at the same time, over the smoking skillet on the stove, he thought that they throve on trouble. The level-headed ones. That was, her smile seemed to say, what they were for.

And the level-headed ones did not shoot off their mouths. A part of their game was to wait. Thus at lunch, while Otto "picked at his food," Lola was able to attack a wing and buttered cornbread; and to explain that, though at breakfast she did choose lightbread, at noon she could do with a bit of cornbread, but with fresh butter, hard pressed. She did dislike butter with beads of blue milk still in it. He might never have known, except perhaps from her occasionally longer glance at his square blond head, that she smelled a rat.

How much did she know? he wondered, watching her search over the platter for another wing. Some women could pluck *knowing* out of the air, the way an organ grinder's monkey could pull down a coin that had nearly sped by—and tip its little red hat. This one opposite him at table, with curls beneath her headrag and sweet cheeks turning to jowls—did she know what he hardly knew himself . . . that he had just left a big moist cave; dark; with a rock falling now and then from the roof, echoing into a pool he could not see?

She was in no hurry to say what she knew. Her ankles were substantial; her behind was broad; but so was her tact. She was handling him, skilfully, as she would a child out of whom she intended to get something later. She was leaning back, running her napkin into its ring, sighing, leaning forward to pick up their plates. "Washing up comes first, eh?" she said. "Any stuff left in the sink just baits the roaches."

She had turned on the water. She was holding out a towel. "I wash and you dry," she said, and she calmly saw to it that that took time. She made sure that he had really polished the glasses and did not stack the blue-bordered plates with the red. Even then she was in no haste. She had to have, she said, a moment to give herself a lick; to run a comb through her head and slip into something fresh. The moment, by Otto's time, lasted a quarter of an hour, while he sat in a rocker to one side of the hearth, listening to a half-bred sheep dog thump its tail in a dream.

But when she reappeared, refreshed, she was ready. She took the rocker on the far side of the hearth; dug her plump elbows into her thighs; leaned forward and said, "Better spit it out. What's wrong?"

No doubt such abruptness worked with children; made them jabber with relief; it closed Otto's mouth. He had come to sit at her knee for sympathy; come expressly to talk but, now, with her eyes on his, he could not. How could he tell a grown woman that he had been "thinking blue?" Yet when she did not move or change her expression, he had to do something. He took the plunge.

"I have been 'thinking blue,' " he said.

"Ah," she said, placidly, as if she herself "thought blue" every morning, just after coffee; so that he was able to bolt on, like a child. "The picture fell off the wall," he said. "The one of my folks. It hit the floor. It broke their faces."

"Ah!" she said again and picked up a cat from the outer ashes between the andirons and held up its head to scratch its chin. "A shame!" she added. "I expect you favored your Pa, at least in the face."

Her voice was soft with more pity than he thought she would feel for a man whose only trouble was a lost picture. Her eyes, while she stroked the cat, roamed about the room slowly, darker, with a look of patience and reservation. She had tucked aside questions about his phrase "thinking blue." She would get into that, but into a great deal else too. Not now; later; in due time; possibly when his guard was down. So her blue eyes said.

Meanwhile, light slanted into the room from the open gallery door. Shadows of leaves moved over the linoleum. A Dominecker hen stepped in on her chapped toes which clicked on the floor, looking for cornbread crumbs beneath the table.

Lola felt under the cat's chin. She let the hen peck. "Blue," she said then. "By that you didn't have in mind what we mean by 'having the blues,'" and nodded when he answered emphatically, "No. Not that."

"I made certain you didn't," she said. She waited, as if not to let the hen hear, until the hen had left, and, soothingly, (she did not want to get "crossways" with him) asked if she might ask two questions.

"Yes," he said.

"First," she began, obviously not referring to his hump because she frankly tapped her brow, "was your people good healthy folks?" And taking his puzzled silence for assent, went on. "Don't you get hurt now," she said. "I just happened to wonder if you ever took a drop; a little drop, say, before breakfast?"

"No," he said, this time angrily. "I have a beer with my sandwich at lunch . . . . She held up a hand. "Sandwich!" she said, and with motherly clucks and swellings said, "That may be it. You don't eat right!"

She repeated that no lone man knew how to eat, before he could go on—on to say that he drank nothing else except perhaps a whiskey before supper.

"Well then," she said, "your folks was sound and you don't do morning drinking. And yet you say you 'think blue.' A lot of people would call the wagon if they heard that."

He said nothing. That was also his opinion. That was why he had come here. For a while she also was silent. The hen had left her droppings on the top step of the gallery and hopped out to a row of lilacs under clumps of apple trees, old and stunted, along the property line.

"Blue, blue, blue," Lola said then. "If that's your Dutchman's way, after all, of 'having the blues,' you've got company. I have 'em all the time. Think about me. Think of being born like everybody else and having to live in a house like this, and treated by the town as if you smelled bad. Think of meeting a man on the street with his wife, and him not speaking to you."

"That is not what I meant at all," Otto said.

"It's what *I* mean," she said easily. "Furthermore, what I think is, you've got things mixed up. I think you've got the blue air over that lake and the waterfalls you keep talking about all balled up with a common fit of the 'blues.' Now you take down from where I come from. . . ."

Otto interrupted. "That," he repeated, "is not what I meant at all."

But she would not listen. She wanted to tell him about where she came from; a country which she vaguely named as Carter County and down around there.

"I take it our hills is lower than yours, alps they tell me you call them, but you'd find ours blue enough to suit you. They stand up, line after line of them, with blue air in between. Lord God," she said, "take a hot misty noon, with everything smelling of cedars and a good cow shed."

He would have spoken but it was as if, having begun, she could not stop. "We lived in a double cabin with a dog run," she said. "Down a bit below that was a spring house. A water bobbed out of it so cold and so strong that a gander couldn't swim it, not up to where we set the milk to cream up." As if she'd been repeating something she'd learned, she went on. The spring stream splashed into a river a few rods away. The river was white in the riffles, but made blue water under bluffs; under cliffs with fern and seedlings of a thing you called columbine in the ledges. You had to watch for copperheads in all that rock, that warm rock. They lay in a kind of mushy circle, but they could strike like fire . . . .

A sort of pleasant wonder had come over her face, but she saw Otto's lifted hand and stopped. When he'd said again that that was not what he meant, she gave the cat a long stroke from nape to tail and invited him to say what he did mean. "If you can do it," she added. "What I think now," she went on sagely, "is that you don't know, yourself. Why don't you just talk on and on, no matter what, and talk it out?"

He rocked in his chair; she in hers; twirls of air about the andirons lifted up ash from the last burning; he wondered if talk could help. Would it not amount to a monologue spoken to the wall behind her? By her own account, she had had parts of two terms in a log-built school, where she had learned to add and subtract, but had been confirmed in the odd "English" she'd known from birth. He, on his side, had finished his communal course, in which his two . . . his even three . . . native languages had been corrected and nourished and where he had even received a certain dosage of Latin—lives of the saints with even scraps of the saints' works, which had pleased him so that he remembered them; recalled them as humble Americans could recite passages of the Preamble of the Constitution. He rocked in his chair, and asked himself if she could understand what he *did* mean, and she saw that in his eyes.

"You talk high and mighty," she said, "but you go on. Take your time. I can get your meaning from your voice. With you," she added, "a yard dog could do that."

Probably she saw that her last words vexed him. Probably she had said them to do that, to prick him on in a pouting if need be. Anything to get him into motion. He drew a breath and, in a bit out of spite, he said:

"I remember it well from school. A man named Saint Augustine said something like this, that Time does not die; it hangs on into the present; it shapes up the future."

"Your boy," Lola interrupted, "had something

on the ball there. Not that we had any saints in our church. I mean Poppa's church. Poppa was the preacher. Yes," she added, seeing Otto stare, "he had him a little slab-sided church up in the woods. Piny woods. With an organ that when anybody pumped it, it set the jays to yelling for miles around."

She hesitated, groping for words. "I can see," she continued, "what your man meant by Time not standing still. Even around here now, as old as I am, whenever I hear a jaybird bawling 'Thief! Thief!', I smell hymn books and pine tar. Like a pie in the oven. All at one and the same time."

"Then you know," Otto said, over the wind humming in the flue between their chairs, "what I mean by 'thinking blue'."

"Baby talk," she said.

"Then you know," he went on, unmoved, "what happened today when the picture fell. I *heard* my mother's skirts as she knelt down at the stove. I *felt* my father's mouth, down in his beard, when he kissed me goodnight."

"Our Pa was saved," Lola said. "He would not have kissed anybody; that would have been of the earth, earthy. Not that he would leave Momma alone even during her periods; she told me once."

Lola rocked back and forth, her heels tapping hard when they hit the floor. Her eyes, looking straight ahead at Otto, seemed not to see him. "Momma was a frail little stub of a woman," she said, "almost humpbacked from all that childbirth and all that wash. Washing clothes . . . wringing out blankets and over-halls . . . There was no end to it.

"She had a tub set up on three rocks out by the dog run, where she could see the hills whenever she straightened up and put a hand to the small of her back. I expect she was 'thinking blue,' by the baby talk you make up."

Lola was rocking faster, her face flushed with anger; anger with her father or any other man, perhaps even with Otto himself.

"Momma never got to go any place," she said, "except to 'services' or maybe a funeral. Sundays, she would put on her dress and we'd all of us pile in the wagon; us girls and the boys except the little one which he died at the age of three and she put a Mason jar full of Christmas tinsel on his grave."

Otto did not know how to continue. It was hard to keep a woman on a subject, maybe not worthwhile trying. But when Lola stopped for breath, he said rapidly, "Yes, yes, but to get back. To get back to 'thinking blue.' It's not the thing itself, but the way it happens that makes me nervous."

"You don't get decent meals," she said. "You live off of trash."

His eyes moved about the room, as if he were to find his next thought amidst the catsup bottles on the table. But by now he was determined to get on. "It's like a nightmare," he said finally, "but a nightmare right in the day time, in the sunlight; really a *mare*, or some kind of unnatural animal, a freak, but friendly, even affectionate." He laughed apologetically, seeing that Lola was smiling, but said, "Wait! It's like, it's like the cloth horse, at the circus, that prances about with the clowns; the black plush horse with the white eyeballs and the red gums, that jumps and capers and bends its body in the wrong places . . . Only, in Mrs. Lightfoot's room it makes my hair stand on end when it puts its jaw in my lap and looks up at me."

Lola was still rocking, still smiling. "I've been to the circus too," she said. But suddenly she sat still and her round face grew serious.

"You folks that live off to yourselves so much," she said, "take to thinking that everything that happens to you is peculiar. You for instance . . . you set there and tell me how the past comes back on you, alive. You hear your Momma's skirts and you feel your Daddy's whiskers." She snorted; said, "Pshaw!"; and asked, "How'd you like to be in my shoes? How'd you like to feel your Pa going over your head with a stick of stove wood, raising blood up under your hair—as he did, because I let a boy kiss me?"

Her eyes were hooded and old for a moment. She moved her lips as if she had been chewing.

"Jim Henderson was the boy's name," she said. "From off the next place. And he'd come at me whenever I was slopping hogs at our pen which was a piece away from the house in a stand of oak . . . . Oh, I let him kiss me all right. I done worse. You know what a girl is. And he was taller than most. A bean pole. And had the longest eyelashes of any man in this world."

She resumed her rocking, muttering, "He was so big I thought I had to have him," but speaking so faintly that Otto felt that he might interrupt—when she abruptly said, out loud, "Pa shot Jim one night."

"Anyway," she added, seeing Otto start, "Pa got up from behind a rock and shot *at* him and he fell.

How was I to know that he was not layin' there with his face blown off? How was I to know that Jim was quick enough to spin around and fall in the oak mast and just get a few shot in his back? How was I to know *anything*, with Pa jerking me home by one elbow, not even letting up when I fell to my knees? . . . Home!" Lola laughed. "At home he got him a piece of hickory out of the wood shed. He hit me all around the head and shoulders, the way you would beat a boy. He mashed the goods of my dress down into my shoulders. He was saving my soul."

Otto kept silent, rocking gently himself in his own rocker and averting his eyes. He had had no way of knowing that he would provoke memories so savage. Anyway, Lola was going on.

"They put me on a pallet out in the dog run," she said. "For a few days there, nobody knew if I could see or hear. As for seeing, I don't know; my eyes was swole shut; Momma kept rubbing goose grease on them. But as for hearing," she added, loudly and viciously almost, to Otto, as if he had been to blame, "do you know what I kept hearing over and over then, then and now—you with your plush horse?"

He had no chance to answer. She was already saying, "In the dog run on the pallet, with the hounds licking the grease off my face, what I kept hearing was that shot that Pa shot; the buckshot biting through the oak leaves; tearing off Jim Henderson's face."

She half weeping and wiping her nose, pointing at Otto with her free hand. "Did you hear me say that I *heard* the rip then *and* now?" she asked. "I still do hear it. I still do feel the shot in the flabby part of my arm. I spill the juice of a berry pie . . . I jerk about and drop things. If you and your mare and your saint whatsomever his name is, think you are alone in this, you can go to hell in a handbasket."

She found nothing else to say. She rocked, grasping her chair arms. Otto thought of nothing to ask. For a long while they sat, guardedly silent as if they had quarreled. The sun had completely left the gallery outside. From the other direction; from behind the kitchen door which led out to the entry way, they caught the hum and murmur of girls "getting ready"; of their crowding and giggling, their squeals over nothing. Some of them, dressed, were already down in the big room with the bead-fringed lamps and the trilling pianola. They were singing. Before Lola stirred, Otto caught a verse:

> "*I want a girl, just like the girl*
> *That married dear old dad.*
> *She was a pearl, the only only girl*
> *That daddy ever haa—aa—aad!*"

There were spills of laughter; sounds of jovial shoving, while the pianola, shaking even in its wooden case, bleated an intermezzo.

Otto was inclined to see it as almost innocent, like the scuffling of school girls on their way to class. Lola took it otherwise. "The bitches," she said, "will tear the place apart. Something comes over them. I'll have to comb my head and get out there."

Otto rose to let her go by. He and she, at least on nights when he was present, had hit upon a division of tasks.

She, once dressed, went to light a cone of incense inside the big-bellied heathen in the hall; tidied up the big pink room with the lamps, and "saw to" the girls.

He, meanwhile walked out for a turn in what they called "the back of the place." He locked the henhouse; poked into the woodshed for prowlers, and made encouraging sounds to the watchdog, a blue tick bitch. He so liked her wet nose in his hand and the wiggle of her whole body along his leg. He so liked stopping for a breath of cool air in the vegetable patch. He so liked the smell of bark and leaves that came up from everywhere, moist, as dusk fell . . . . He would have even liked to find, as the hens had, rustling and clucking their last clucks, a perch of his own in this quiet place.

It was a pity that Lola felt grim about her own share of the duties. He knew she did, though she never said that she would prefer the smell of apple bark to that of incense and of the broadcloth of the gentlemen who arrived to pass the evening. She never said anything. She merely left the kitchen with blank, determined eyes and thin lips, and did not return . . . to undress, groaning, when he was already in bed.

Usually she had already gone out through the mauve-colored hall into the pink room, when he came in from latching up the hens. Tonight she was still there in the kitchen, dressed and ready, with a high comb in her back hair, but apparently waiting to speak with him. He stopped, surprised, and let her walk up close to him without touching her.

"Do you know," she asked in a rapid undertone, "why I told you all that stuff about me and my folks and Jim Henderson?" And before he could shake his head, she said, "It was to show you that you're not the only one who can 'think blue.' I do it too. More women do it, I expect, than men; more women than the usual run of men; anyway the dummies in pants that I have to deal with."

He stepped back, farther away from her. Having just heard the hens, and stood in the nice normal twilight between the turnips, he did not wish to be reminded that he was not of the usual run of men. But she followed him as he drew away. She stood close, looking up squarely while she squarely said, "You've got that hump on your back. No use in us beating about the bush."

He looked away to avoid her eyes, but she reached up for his ears and pulled his head about until she could kiss him on the mouth. "That's where we start at," she said. "At that hump."

He closed his eyes. He let her do the embracing. If she chose to be blunt about his disfigurement, all very well. But he was not going to help her with it. He only smiled to himself when she said that, to her way of thinking, a hump might make a man more gentle; might make him more sensitive—smiled because she had said "sinsitive" for "sensitive."

And yet, at that, he felt himself stiffen in her embrace. Something beyond his senses suggested that she was not talking idly, that, above all, she had merely halted. She had not stopped for good. What made him grow rigid between her arms was his conviction that he had already heard what she was about to say. Exactly what it was he could not tell, but he already *remembered* it, as he remembered the sound of a rock falling from a cave roof or dropping from the ledge of a cliff, hitting ledge after ledge before it spun out into space where hearing could not follow it.

The excitement made him grasp her tightly by the waist—the more firmly because she had pulled his head down to where she could rub her nose against his.

"Why," she asked, and smothered her face against his shirt front, "don't you go back to Mrs. Lightfoot's now; tonight; this minute, and fetch your traps and come live with me?"

IV

THE CRICKETS, THAT AUTUMN, WERE AS loud as frogs. Nights shone clear. The days were full of a kind of standing mist, blue, though the sun was bright. Frost came early, so that the maples turned pink and yellow, and elms let down their leaves though there was no wind. The walnut trees, almost bare themselves, dropped nuts that bounced against their branches. Then the days and nights, both, turned warmish. The girls of the house called this time an Indian summer.

Otto left his shop which he had now taken in the High Street as soon as four o'clock of an afternoon, and limped home fast, hurrying to get at tasks that, as Lola said, never got done before the snow, "without" there was a man about the place. Something would have gone wrong with the chickenhouse latch; there would be kindling to split; the guineas persisted in roosting in trees where the owls could knock them down; the grass might need sickling for a last time.

Lola would come out to watch him, wearing an old hat of his own; with a sweater dangling from her shoulders; warming her hands under her arms against the settling frost. She would warn him not to do too much, but gloat over what he did. Small things seemed to please her excessively. Once when she found him planing off a lid to keep squirrels out of his barrel of walnuts, she said, "You'll get that back." He looked up; examined her whole bosomy little figure standing in the dusk, curiously. Her voice had sounded choked. And she was going on. She was saying, almost in the tones of a woman offering grace, "There'll be nights with us sitting with our knees to the fire; with us cracking nuts on flat irons; filling us a fruit jar." And she added that, to her mind, nothing smelled better than walnut meats in winter. "Unless it's hickory smoke, easing around your back in a chilly room."

He believed it, feeling the glow that met them when they went in to supper; into the dark kitchen where the floor was dancing with reflections from vents in the firebox; where the air, the rocker cushions, possibly even the fur of the drowsing cats, already smelled of winter smoke.

Once inside, Lola had no time. She was obliged to get herself up; to go out on the job; to be everywhere at once, keeping order. Exactly where and when, she never knew. Mr. Blitzstein was usually quiet; he was content to impress his Negress with a semblance of evening clothes. But Mr. Ware-Harington for instance, meek as he looked; small with a walrus moustache, liked odd sports with his girl, who liked them too but who screamed. And there were the police themselves, boys really, with flushed faces and pushed-back caps, who were frequently louder than their elders who fell out of bed and complained that they had lost their wallets. It was a great strain. And year after year, as Lola said.

But there Otto helped, too. There he did some really "odd jobs" for a man about the place. He had, say, when he'd come from the shop, slid a pork roast into the stove (of which the fire never quite went out). Thus she often had, when she came out of the bedroom, with beads and leather shoes and a rhinestone comb, nothing to do but make a salad as he had taught her to do and break up a *baguette de pain* that he had brought home from Monroe Street.

After that, he could not assist her. The other part of the house had come to be, for him, like a railway station that he happened to live next door to. It was as if, at ten-fifteen, an express shook the panes. Shortly then (but he had dozed off), a local puffed to a stop; he heard the hiss. But he could do nothing about cars that slid past or bumped and humped on rails under sheds. He had learned to drop off to sleep.

Lola shook him awake. Coming into what even she now called "home"; yawning after work and letting a nightgown down about herself, she pulled him over to her side of the bed and hugged him, and ran her fingers through his chest hair.

She did not like his phrase "being hygienic," though he explained it to her carefully. After a pause under the eiderdown that was broad enough for both, she stated that there was more to it than that. "At least," she said, letting another long rest go by, "there is a heap more to it for folks like us."

And he could not contest it. When they had finished with one another; when they lay, breathing against one another in the mid-sag of the feather bed; when she, either as a maternal gesture or simply as the easiest way to lie, turned him over and took his hump between her breasts, there did seem to be, as she said, "more to it."

Such nights, or those of them that remained with

him more keenly, were moonlit nights; nights of a whiter, rounder moon, when they lay with just their noses out from under the covers, and talked.

They talked, that was it. Sometimes they mumbled and dozed off; or they spoke clearly but disconnectedly, trusting each other to jump the gap. It was, in the foggy moonlight, as if they had known one another all their lives.

He would tell her, *à propos* of *what* he did not know, how the little girls had squealed at his spider's scramble up the rocks; his climb up to where he could watch them all unseen. And she, on the upturn of a snore, vowed there was nothing bitchier than a girl in her first long skirts. Give her a boy any time. Even a Jim Henderson. Had she ever told him about Jim Henderson? When she finished the snore, but did not go on, seeming to start awake and wait, he wished to tell her about waterfalls. There had been waterfalls everywhere you looked, when he was a boy. But why waterfalls? What had they to do with girls or with a boy he'd never known?

The zaniness of it unexpectedly eased him. It was as if he had been able to dry up pockets of pus about his person, or prick out the water of blisters. Maybe the women had been right all along—with their gabbling on and on, aimlessly; their dealing out information like random hiccoughs? Perhaps men, at least men like himself who tried to force thought into the sausage-gut of logic, had missed the sausage? Also the logic? At any rate the easement from tight-wire tension?

Be that as it might, the fact was that he wished to tell Lola about waterfalls. He felt the spray of them on his face while she, with a wiggle like the wiggle of the hound in the garden, placed her whole length along his back.

At home, he said to her, or to the rays of moonlight on the coverlid, you were, in the first place, rarely out of sight of a waterfall. Anywhere you looked you saw them, each falling straight until it hit a foaming and a beady, thundering foot on the rock. Some of them shot out so far off from the top stone that you dared walk under the moving wall it made, where everything was flash and roar and something seemed to be sucking away the breath from your mouth. And Lola would say, "Law! That would be a wonder in this world!"

The notion of wide air and water bemused her. She had always felt gagged and strangled if she remained long in any house; in any kind of house whatever. Her dream was to live out where there was always wind, or anyway a breeze, in her hair and under her armpits; and with some rolling water off just yonder, somewhere close.

With him it was just the other way around. Wind made him restless and apprehensive. And as for space and empty air, he wanted her to know how teetery it made you feel when you stood on the cliff at home and looked across at the cathedral and the mountains, or, worse, down at the birds. The birds flew by with businesslike steadiness, in cross formations, one group hundreds of feet below the other, all of them over the gravelly bend of a tiny river with four tiny fir trees on one bank of a curve and one on the other. The sight of it made him sick and seemed to pull him forward. He still, at the thought of it under the covers, shivered so that Lola kissed his hump and pulled the covers up over him.

Meanwhile, in the frosty moonlight that showed one's breath, she did not let him do all of the talking. She evidently felt the same release that he got out of sleepy and apparently aimless chatter; and she wanted him to know that she had been born in a cabin chunked with straw and cow dung; two cabins really, with a dog run in between. It was up high, as far up as that country allowed. She laughed. You knew that by a feel in the air . . . the air that smelled of cedar and pennyroyal. And anyway, the men always built on a ridge. Carrying wash water up from the creek was women's work. Not even the women questioned that.

But oh, she went on, when the men came up the hill, even they, on that steep grade, had to use the stock path. Talk about hairpin curves! Sometimes one line of the mounting track was only three or four feet above the line below it (all in the pennyroyal!). The word was, in the country, that deer and elk had cut out those ways before cows were thought of. She did love cows though. Their mule ears; their pointed hip bones; their big, warm veiny bags; their trot when they got to a level.

One night she said:

"I can't think to my soul why I remember Pa on one special day back then, but I do recollect him coming up that stock path, which it was almost a gully, bent-kneed and slow. He did everything slow. Even in the pulpit he acted like he was sighting down a rifle . . . He was a thin man, with a black hat and a dark face though he shaved on Saturdays.

His eyes were black too; set close, and looked like they was looking past your legs at something you couldn't see even if you whipped around to look. Naturally he had a gun slung under his arm (a man then would rather go out without his pants); and naturally with some dead game bobbing around his belt. Two squirrels that day and one dove. I mind the blood running out of the dove's beak onto his hip. Maybe that's why I remember it." And she added after a moment, for no reason that Otto could trace, "What with him running on and on about the Blood of the Lamb."

But that was the good part of such talking, or blathering if you wished to call it that. There was no reason in looking for reasons. With their muscles loose and their minds off guard, they were both simply skimming at random over the top of things which, in the daylight, they'd say they did not remember. Probably it was the surest way to get at the truth, if the truth of such trifles mattered.

Yet sometimes it was not a trifle that emerged. One night, for instance, Lola, brought half awake by her own hoarse breath, said, "Keep on talking. I'm listening." But Otto had not been speaking; he had been asleep. She had dreamed that he was telling her something, and—this interested Otto enough to waken him completely—whatever that was lay athwart something else she was dreaming. Something stronger. Because she said how odd it was that he had never asked her how she had ever got into such a house as the house she lived in now. That was peculiar. She thought all gentlemen were dead to know how a girl had got into a house.

Her voice was perhaps indistinct at the edges. Part of the time she had a quilt pulled over her face. Now and then she mumbled. But, in the still, cold room, her worded dream could be put together.

The night Poppa had shot Jim, or shot at Jim, Poppa had led her home and stopped before the woodshed to get out a length of hickory. "He whupped me slow, all about the head and shoulders, the way he would beat a boy. He mashed the dress goods down into my skin. To save me from the fire. He kept saying that."

But the thrashing had not worked. Jim had light-brown eyes and was taller than the run of boys. Slim in the hip. With a grip in his fingers. And bold! The night they had run off together, he had stopped the train. Flagged it down somehow.

She had never been close up to such a thing. But there it was. All the cars halted on a bend, shaking in the smoke, and the engine with one eye so bright that she saw small green weeds in the roadbed, but could only feel the heat of the machine itself, so that Jim had had to lead her inside like a blind girl, to find a seat. At the fourth stop they got down. Landed at a considerable settlement, to judge by the lights and the racket; just where, it seemed like, you had to step over a lot of shiny, curved track to reach a hotel called the Blossom House. In there she and Jim, by the kindness of a manager, who was bald but had sideburns, were given a room to themselves.

For Otto, this beginning was like the set start of a folk tale. The middle section would have variations. But the end, whether you heard it in English or French or German, perhaps even Russian or Chinese, would return to a formula.

Sure enough, Jim was gone in the morning when she waked up, terrified to be alone in a strange room where there were pillow slips on the pillows and the puffing of trains below the window. He had even taken the thirty-five cents she had earned at picking blackberries, which she had left on a doily that covered a table by the bed. She could still see the stitch of the doily.

And sure enough the manager, the ogre in this American version, had come in while she was still in bed and vowed that he would not mention to the police what was due on the room, if she cared to work out the amount in some other way. He was even so thoughtful as to let her wash dishes in the hotel for her keep for some months on, which she did, because she knew that she might as well stand in front of one of the speeding engines outside as to go home. And, in the end, she had not known whether the baby was Jim's or the manager's. What she did know was that it had sort of smiled once—pulled back its lips—and could spread its toes like its fingers and smelled like milk. Also that it had died.

She had had it in the house of a woman down the tracks, where the manager had placed her. A motherly soul who, when the baby died, had put her into this present house. In this present house where, timid at first, she had gradually asserted herself (perhaps she had a bit of Pa in her, in reverse) until now she could tell the rest of the women "where to set their buckets."

She was talking, talking, talking; now in a nearly natural voice, nearly awake; now in a low and confused and weeping jumble. He made note of the idiom about buckets; he liked idioms generally and it behooved him to learn the local ones. He also heard her weeping. Because of that he managed to turn around in bed, which was painful for him, and kiss her, and she patted his face. But the great point for him, the point which, in spite of the warm depth of the featherbed, made the hair of his neck stand up, was that he had caught her in the act of "thinking blue."

Indeed she was still at it in the morning. Her turning-and-folding of the breakfast dough was mechanical. She could do that and yet smell the baby's breath and watch him move his toes apart. For Otto, pulling on his work shirt and getting into his corduroys, that was plain from her sleepwalker's motions; from her "working" the dough without looking down at it.

And he knew what was coming. At the table, with the stove glowing and taking off the chill; with lamplight falling across the catsup bottles in the middle of the oilcloth, over the eggs and rolls and a dish of damson preserves, she talked on as she had done in bed.

What she probably saw, dimly in the motes over the lamp, was the outline of a man's big square blond head—his own. What *he* got—but clearly, because this time it was she who was "thinking blue"—was the sight of a woman whose wrinkles looked deeper in that light; whose thick braids lay one on each shoulder of her kimono and who had taken up a kitten into her lap. Ordinarily she would not have done that at the table. The creature was white, with hardly-weaned weak blue eyes; soft, furry, and curious to tap its foot into her plate and look back up at her. He doubted if she really saw it. She was saying:

"The woman in that house down by the tracks seemed to know her business. She tied a knotted sheet to the bottom of the bed for me to pull on. She was right there to wipe off the sweat." After a moment she added, as if she had been giving a new proof of the woman's skill, "There was a persimmon tree outside that window. It lit up, whenever them locals went by. Them locals shook the bed."

Otto ate just enough so as not to draw her attention. But it was hard to swallow and he kept dropping his napkin. For a reason that he could not fix but which he almost resented, he felt that she was drawing him into her own "blue thinking." That should be her own task. Why should he, who had troubles of his own, shake with beads of sweat in the hair between his knuckles while he groped about for the napkin? Oh but he did. He felt the baby's breathing; saw the rictus which Lola had taken for a smile; and most distinctly of all heard the steel squeak of the local, rounding a bend outside and, with its big eye, causing the persimmon tree to jump at him out of the dark.

"She held the baby up by the feet for me to see," Lola was saying, to him or to the kitten. "He was peekid, though."

*   *   *

Otto got up and got out, leaving her humped over the drawstring of her nightgown yoke. She was staring into the lamp globe, missing the cat when she tried to stroke it. It was playing with a piece of ham rind on her plate.

He needed air. He wanted the effort of flapping his bad foot up the hill. Welcomed the struggle in the keen, neutral morning air and welcomed the drop of his key in the lock and the feel of his door knob. The door of his shop in the High Street, which was hardly a shop—a booth, really; a narrow, timber, splintery space twittering with movements and ticks, with here and there a tinny strike of the hour. A place where a man might hope to settle wrongs with a drop of oil, or the twist of a doll-sized screwdriver, pushed into the right groove. He would, here, re-man himself, so to speak, and help Lola later.

＊   ＊   ＊

He thought he had a chance that night. He found her combed and dressed, ready to go out and see to the girls. And she had got supper; spoon bread and greens, with a duck he had brought her the day before. But there, as they sat at the table, were her blue eyes; vague; not appearing to see the lamp-wick. And there was her voice, mumbling and muted, while she ran from subject to subject, with no connection to follow. "Cows," she said, for instance, and laid down her knife.

She did purely love cows. Even what with scalding the buckets and churning and all of that. Think of their big mule ears; their hip bones; their veiny bags. It was sweet to hear them nuzzling about after the bran in their feed box. She even liked the smell of their flanks. She had always wanted one of her own.

"But the council," Otto objected, as gently as he could, "would probably not let us keep a cow in town."

"No," she said humbly after a moment, "the council would not allow us a cow in a place like this. I know that well enough."

He looked up sharply. Something—something rather more in his hump than in his mind—had pricked him into attention. The moment had been calculated. He felt that. Her voice had been intended to sound grim, not humble; her eyes, with swollen pupils, fixed his precisely but ever so briefly, in a bit of smoke over the lamp chimney. She was, if he knew women, "making a point" without, she hoped, having to spell it. It was a way they had. Often a useful shortcut. Frequently he got the signal.

But not tonight. Or apparently not. Surely not. He squinted past the bright heat of the lamp off into the kitchen; at the rockers, the rag rugs, the sleeping cats and polished andirons; and wondered who, in his right mind, (having fought his way to this snug nook) would trade so much as one dying pulse of the stove for, of all things, a cow somewhere away?

He had missed the message, if there had been one. And what puzzled him more and more painfully was the length of time that Lola took to "think blue." With him it came on in spells, like the pinch in a hip joint during a rain, or in a run of misty days. An old complaint that came and went (sometimes even companionably after you were fifty). But now here she did not leave off; kept picking up needles when she wanted spools and all but walked into closed doors; went on munching and staring past bedposts while she pulled on her stockings. Day after day.

Was she in fact "thinking blue" or was she physically ill and trying not to distress him until she had to? He ran over the short list of what he could throw together as "female troubles": irregular periods—surely Lola was over that kind of thing; fallen womb—no; unexplained migraines—no. Lola was not a person to lie with a wet cloth over her brow and the shades pulled down . . . . But what of a lump on her breast? He could not find one, but women—like cows that graze where their calf is *not* hiding—knew about such things.

The stout ones did not tell, but deserved any easement a wretched male (with nothing but an enlarged prostate) could give her.

The idea had at least this merit, that it gave him something to do. By night he tried to sleep lightly; if there was a cackling in the henhouse, he rose and went to see why, without being asked. Mornings, he made sure that all of the stoves of the house were free of ash and clinkers. By coming home early, he made time to repair all of the furniture that stuck or wobbled and once, when, as daylight grew longer, he repainted all of the girls' rooms—of a color which Effie called "tittie pink." Effie, still called "The Wink," for reasons which Otto no longer wished to go into, refused him entrance to her quarters, fresh paint or none. He had been, she said, a prompt-paying fellow but he had deserted her, and for a woman that practically had grey hair, at that.

When a windy late March had brought out a choked row of old daffodils, just this side of the apple trees and clumps of lilac, a few yards from the rail of the kitchen gallery, he took off a whole Saturday and spaded up the garden. It was a mixed plot, a vegetable patch, really, between the bedroom window and the privies, except for a row of marigolds and another of zinnias; but large enough, between its hedges of berry bushes, to tax him. It was sharp work, to stand upon his good foot and shoot down the spade with his bad one, keeping balance and stopping to mop his brow.

He was glad to halt at intervals, when Lola stepped out wearing another of his old hats; feeling of her elbows under a sweater and raising her nose as if, in her life, she had never sniffed anything like daffodils and new apple leaves and blossoms almost out.

It was pleasant to have her there, crossing her hands over her stomach and saying "Law!" when she saw how many rows he had spaded up, each lying against another, glinting slightly.

But it was nice to see her go back inside, too, with the sleeves of her sweater dangling; humping her back when she felt for the rail to pull herself up. Her praise was good. But so was being alone— with the almost physically exciting downward push of the spade; the distant honks of motor cars in the High Street; the private talk of a mockingbird under the new apple leaves; and the late, cool breeze that lifted his hair.

Once, soothed by it all, he went to sit upon a bench; a wooden one that backed into the berry bushes hedging the patch. He did so, so he'd have said, to muse and rest; but he kept on smelling the turned earth and hearing the bird; and sat up alert.

Late as it had got, the Roman egg of the capitol dome still rose, white on the west side, far away to his left. It was strange to see this Italian-looking thing planted on the bank of a broad American river, throwing its shadow (as it might well be doing at that moment) over stern-paddle steamers which were making upstream from spots with names like Cairo and Cape Girardeau. And yet what else could the Americans build when they wished a seat of law? An Indian tepee, with a calico pony tethered near it, would not do either . . . and he dismissed that.

His eye was rather more taken anyway by the lamps coming on, away to his right, in the penitentiary; a vague bulky mass with towers still rising into the light, over blank lengths of wall. That was the law, too, but visibly more active; visibly and intimately active (the lights kept pricking on, one above two; three beneath four); intimately more active under men's swinging arms and in the sound of their coarse leather tread . . . . And now he, a twisted thing, *un avorton* as the boys at home had called him; he, who had no proper business with ideas, nevertheless felt that he was about to have one . . . an idea. It would be a simple one no doubt; one that normal people had had over and over. But he could not resist it. It beat in his blood pulse, in time with the *eins zwei, eins zwei, eins zwei* of the brogans off yonder where the convicts were marching in from the prison farms to chow.

He heard, or he felt, the feet; the short step, marking time; the swinging away from a halt. He plainly saw faces, pink or black loops in the line, and the white of eyeballs watching, out of the loops, for a change in the tilt of the guard's rifle. Now they broke lines, at command, to wash; now, *hup*, one two three, they had reached a high hall that smelled of ham hock and molasses: now at command they stopped beside tables, the far ends of which seemed to join, like points in a perspective: now, in single file, they trod to seats before their plates—but there they were not to talk. They winked at the next man when they wanted the salt passed.

And in their silence full of motions, Otto had his little idea. Some of the men were swine who belonged where they were; some, let us say, could be martyrs; all, like himself, had been squeezed into places where their respective humps might roughly (give or take a piece of broken skin) be made to fit. Grant that. But his idea, which he now thought great, was that fellows so constricted (and as he himself was) might, by that very fact, achieve a sort of liberty; a strange, a rare kind of freedom that nobody could take away because nobody else could see it. It was mysterious, as religious mysteries are mysterious, if you liked; and yet you could get at it by roundabout ways. Think for in-

stance of a fountain—how, because it rises from a
narrow split like the reed of a clarinet, it sends up
a higher stalk of water, and casts a wider floating
of mist out over the mignonette and the moonvine
blooms in a dusky garden.

He stopped at that and grinned, grimly at first
and then with amusement. Frankly, the mignonette
was lacking. What he smelled was the henhouse;
the chicken coops and the privies of—why not get
out the word while he was thinking of other institu-
tions—the privies of a whorehouse.

For a moment he was checked, then smiled
again, widely. The smells that he actually smelled,
as over against those of white lilacs and lilies swaying under moths in the beady air around the fountain, proved exactly what he'd meant. He folded his
bad leg under him and settled back on the bench,
satisfied. Furthermore, what was so wrong about
the odor of a good, practicing henhouse; or that of
the turned earth just behind him; or that of the town
which, all around the base of his hill, was coming
on alight for supper and sending up woodsmoke?

Hickory; chiefly hickory with some oak, he believed. He had found his fountain, here, he thought.
He sighed and sat more solidly down with his foot
under him on the bench, and thought, as if he had
taken a vow in church, "I will never leave this place.
Not while I live. Never. No matter what happens."

At the same time, he saw that he had better do
his thinking and his vowing fast. Lola was coming
down the steps.

Her opening of the kitchen door had made a gash
of light in what was, now, really night. He had not

thought of the time. She had. Things were turning dry on the stove. She was out of patience. She was coming to get him, just for supper, but to get him. Partly because of that (though he could not think why) and partly because, bobbing over the turf in her long skirt and carrying, of all things, a lamp, she put him in mind of some sort of priestess, beaded and belled, caparisoned and ready to call out an incantation. He shrank back on his bench, even pushing his hump into the berry brambles behind him, and resolved not to tell her about the fountain and the white lilacs.

It was instinctive, but childish too. Especially when she got close up and raised up the lamp to see his face. She was no vestal, crowned with mistletoe; no Aztec wheeling a blade in the air—simply old Lola wearing his smashed grey hat, and with her usual local tongue on her.

Some people, she said, didn't seem to have the sense God gave a goose. Some people, just in an undershirt, she said, would work up a sweat in the night air, and then sit outside and wonder why they came down with something. Would he please get in, and, though he had not said a word, please shut up?

He had not spoken. He surely had not. He followed her back up the steps, but at the kitchen door let her go on ahead; and, while she tied on her apron, looked around behind him at what he had left. Lights from houses under the hill had come on in such numbers now that they sent a glow up over the outer sides of the apple tree trunks. Above these, off away over the whole town, the separate brightnesses of the penitentiary had merged into one dim, hovering bar. He watched that especially. It belonged to him and to them. It was his and the convicts'. The sight of it quickened him as if he had got a hoarse password . . . some sort of signal that would send him off at a trot to repeat it to a man crouched down in the bushes at the next post.

Lola was patting at the bow of her apron strings when he turned about. It was not the moment to get her in on this. He resolved not to speak. "Be mum," he told himself, with a last sniff of the night air.

V

AS IT HAPPENED, HE COULD NOT HAVE talked with her had he wished to do so. Lola was cross. Facing the stove; rattling pans; exhibiting her back, somehow, rather than just turning it to him, she managed, by that and by her silence and by the sad angle of her head, to convey that she was miffed.

He did not expect to be told why. That was what being miffed meant—keeping still and making the other person guess. And he took the bait. He did wonder, the more because, while she moved to the table, dishing up, her face was, as she herself might say, "puckered up"; wrinkled in a real grief.

That was at least more reasonable. She was not a woman to pout because he had not "noticed" something—a new arrangement of the furniture, say. Hence it was hardly likely that she'd taken offense at his lolling on the garden bench, watching distant lights, until she had had to fetch him. Normally, as a matter of fact, she'd have welcomed a moment away from the grease and heat, to sit beside him and view the lights herself. She was also, at usual times, a woman who said what she meant quickly when she meant it, the way she would pick up a rock to throw at a cat that was about to catch a bird.

It must be something else. Something more than a flash of ill nature. But he held his tongue at supper, letting the lamp smoke rise; waiting and watching; seeing her bite into a roll and look down at it as if she wondered how it had got there; watching and waiting and turning various matters over in his mind.

She was certainly not getting any younger. Perhaps the lamplight brought out the crow's feet about her eyes unfairly. Still she had, as women say, begun to "let herself go." Her topknot slid about on her head and lost hairpins (one had just fallen on the cloth beside her knife). Her shoulders and arms had put on weight; she wanted a new corset. Veins on the backs of her hands stood up. Her cheeks shook—her jowls, you might almost call them because, as women come to age, they often look like old men.

And yet for all of that—it delighted him and made him feel safe because he was able to do so—he was taking her in with affection; with loyal gratitude. Let her drop pins and throw away her corset. She, out of the millions of women on earth, had picked him out and pulled him to herself; had drawn him out of the "lone" that spread like fungus on the clothes of aging fellows who lived "in rooms." She had baked for him; washed his socks out for him; carried his bath water for him in steaming kettles. She had put him down to her table and taken him into her bed when, as he had so long since learned, the sight of his chin and his swaying back made other women suck in a breath, as if they'd seen a roach crawl under a basket.

He bit into a roll on his own side of the lamp and smiled and was all but glad that her knot did weave about and that she had lost her throat line. This would be his chance. Just as, as a woman, she gave up, she would find *him*, "swurging up" (to use one of her own words) at her elbow, stout and willing and for once not just better than nobody. Oh, he had little plans; ways to smarten up the kitchen ell; to quicken and brighten things for her and make her clap her hands like a girl.

Many people might think that he had already done a great deal. The gas bill, the water bill, the grocer's note, the taxes, even the "cut" silently expected at the city hall—all of these he had gradually, as his business thrived in the High Street, taken over. She had let him do it without special thanks—there was no greed in her; no quick reaching; nothing sly—too much hill-country decency in her for that: but she had now and then kissed him as she'd passed him, with no spoken reason, and she had more than once dropped the hint that it was a God's gift to have a man about the house.

Her voice had made that serious, often to his amusement, because she seemed to attach importance to trifles. He rose at night, for instance, and pulled on his britches if a skunk got into the henhouse; put his shoulder to the door while she stood behind him, if a strange knock came; planed off the legs of a table that rattled dishes. All nothing, really. Take his management of the police; the jovial "micks" in blue who crowded into the kitchen. His presence tamed them. They took off their caps to Lola. They called him "cap'n."

She liked that. It was an advance for her when they opened the bread box and the ice chest with a show, at least, of knowledge that others were in the room.

She had even put her arms around him, sweet and melting, when he chased the children away from the front garden. He was half-ashamed to remember it, it had amounted to so little.

It came to this: two neighborhood kids, one with red hair, neither aged more than ten or twelve, had found a way (which Otto secretly admired) to increase their income. Toward dusk when people still assume they have their eyesight, they planted beer bottles on Lola's front steps—bottles upon which gentlemen trod—gentlemen humming, satiated, snapping on their gloves, having had no reason to suppose that they might suddenly shoot out into the air and light upon their elbows in the gravel of the walk, with a snotnose leaning down above them, a child with red hair, knocking the dents out of their hats and offering to call their wives for fifty cents if they were hurt bad.

All Otto had to do was to come at the boys from under a forsythia, with his twisted chin, saying "Ooooh!" and the two had fled. They took the fence (not waiting for the gate) like deer, and doubtless led a better life for three days . . . . Otto could have followed them. But Lola had stopped him and kissed him on both cheeks and baked him a hen. It was a drawn thorn for her. The gentlemen had not liked it and had frightened her. Blitzstein, the one who came in evening clothes to do odd things with his Negress, had threatened to report it. Otto had kissed her in return and pulled her hands down from his shoulders. It had been such a little thing to do.

Watching her now around the lamp—her own

eyes seemed blind—he searched himself, frisked himself roughly; surely there was something more lasting he could do for her. He looked about. There was the stove. It was long and black, and so humped itself up in the middle to accommodate a bulge in the floor that it might, so he had often thought, set the house afire. But it was a delicate matter to offer a woman a new stove, when she knew the drafts as she knew her feet in their slippers and had learned how to time the bread though the oven door did not quite close.

He remained still, since she found nothing to say, and kept his eye travelling about. On the far side of the room there was nothing Lola would allow to be changed—the andirons on the hearth, the cats, the old muzzle-loader over the mantelpiece. But take this other side. Look at this wall. It had been calcimined pink but was now flaking off in white scales. Worse, it was all one thing; blank and stifling. If one could only see out! Lola would be less glum, he was sure, if she felt air and saw birds in the apple trees and, at night, could watch the lights below the hill.

That of course was what he could do for her— put in a window. He had the tools and had put by some money. Some day when she was upstairs counting sheets or correcting a drunken girl; one morning before she could stop him, he would knock a hole in the wall and set in a window—a big wide glassy bow with a ledge for cats and flower pots. Women—they needn't tell him—liked that kind of thing (standing around with their hands on their hips, looking doubtful and saying that they did declare)—and he'd have preferred to gloat a bit; but

Lola had stirred and begun to speak. Begun at any rate to make pensive sounds; thoughtful soft murmurings, addressed to the hot lamp as well as to him, which meant nothing until it occurred to him that she was, for the first time audibly, going on with a conversation, started in her mind.

It was about cows again. She was saying, staring at the lamp globe with blank blue eyes, that she purely loved cows. That was the way it was. She had had a hard life, but, she added, less to him than to the chicken bone which she put down into her plate, it would have helped all along if she could have had a cow of her own—preferably a Jersey with a deer's eyes and her first calf and a good bag on her; teats that stuck out like pot legs. Otto would, she said, finding him on the other side of the lamp, like to hear such a cow snuff around in her bran box, while she was being stripped. It would do him good to feel the calf's thrust across his knees— calves were amazingly strong and had wet, pebbly noses—the calf's hard push to get its muzzle in the bucket. You had your feet in straw and felt the cow's sweet steaming flank against your brow, and that kind of thing made a man out of a dummy.

Otto agreed, dared anyway to nod. He knew the good smell of a stable as well as she did, and the yielding warmth of a bag. Indeed he took such things for granted; wondered only that Lola could talk of them in such a low and shaken voice; and sat, this time bewildered, when she went on, in the same tone, to say that there were not many ivories left on the keys of Pa's organ. Pa's organ in the church. But there were birds outside.

The shift alerted him, because, to judge from her

blind eyes near the lampwick, there had been no wrench for her. Cows, chicken bones, uneven lights pricking over wick, a lamp chimney blackening up towards its top . . . where was the division? One thing did not come after another; all was a part of all.

He knew that too, as well as he knew the hiss of milk in a bucket, and he risked another nod, while she said that the window beside the organ in the piney wood was broken and there were not many ivories left on the keys of Daddy's organ. She played on the black ones. It was bold of her to go there at all, and wicked of her, in that musty smell of hymnals, but she was young and, on the black keys with now and then a white one, she did pick out unholy tunes. The jay birds, outside the triangle missing from the window, heard her and did knee-bends on the pine bough tips, calling "Thief! Thief! Thief!"

"Isn't it funny," she asked, "how a racket will carry through woods in mist after a shower?" She seemed to catch sight of him accidentally on his side of the lamp again and laughed and said, "And after all, all I was doing was to pump out 'Maggie.'" She lifted a finger and, quaveringly but true, she sang back to him:

> "But to me you're as fair
> As you wair, Maggie,
> When you and I wair young!"

He listened with his eyes half-closed, his chin down over his plate, as a man would, out of respect to a singer; but he was not listening so much as pondering; wondering why, even loose in a woolgathering, she so often mentioned her father, as she had just done and as she had, now that he thought of it, frequently done of late.

What had caused the change? But he must not ask her that. He must not. Instead, he let a long moment go by. The purring of the lampwick was louder than their breath. Off on the hearth, the ash of what had been a late spring fire let out a smoky puff. A cat got up from the bricks and stretched and crossed the room with its tail erect. He let it arch its back and press its weight against his leg while he considered. Was Lola not simply meandering, groping about in the dear dead days, not knowing what she did? Half pleased, perhaps, as people so often were, by a sorrow; by a grief set to thrumming in their minds by faded ribbon and old letters in trunks? If so, she could not be blamed. Few women (or men made delicate by wrong vertebrae) ever, to his knowledge, missed that kind of sweet hurt.

Meanwhile he did not like Lola's close stare at the lamp chimney, as if the light of the flame eating the wick could not harm her eyeballs. What he feared; what made him gather his flesh as if a snake had crawled out of a basket near him, was his suspicion that she was not wilfully reminiscing, but "thinking blue."

Making pellets of his bread beside his plate, he recalled that she had taken up his term and laughed at it and said that everyone did it, and she had furnished some chilling details as proof; her mother's pulling up her frail spine over the washtub, holding onto men's pants in the suds, for a look at the cool blue hills: her father's unshaven scowl under his black hat while his feet parted the pennyroyal in the cattle path and the dove bled from its mouth onto the thigh of his overalls.

He had believed her, or had been silenced at any rate by her laughter and jolly pats on his shoulder; by her assurance that his nonsense did not amount to much; that everybody fell into such a way of thinking at times.

And now here was proof before him, in Lola's sightless eyes held so close to the lamp. How different it was when you watched someone else do it! How embarrassing on the one hand, as if you had been spying, peeking at an intimate act; and on the other hand, how *crawly*; how the snake seemed to lift the loose lid of the basket with its flat head, meaning to ease its way up your trouser leg. You wanted to cry out. You could not sit still.

And presently, to test Lola, he spoke to her, gently, the way he might dare address a sleepwalker near the head of a stair. "Were you all by yourself in the church," he asked, "when you played the song on the black keys?"

At least she heard him. At least his murmur came through and drew her—drew her brightly— away from the lamp. Her eyes seemed to locate him, to move aside to where he sat. Her cheeks dimpled. She smiled. She had known he would understand. So it was agreed. This time, she said, there would be no scrub stock. None of your heifers out of the woods; little devils that kicked and had a white patch over one eye. No, sir. She would be a Jersey, with skin like glove leather, and she would munch bran and hold her bag over the bucket like the lady she was.

"A little lady," Lola repeated. "Blood. You can't get around that. Whatever else you have don't count. It's who your daddy was."

She thrust out her hand, feeling amongst the plates and jam pots and the condiment tray, until she found his fingers and squeezed them. He watched her; watched her topknot slip forward; watched her when she smiled, awkward and shy, like a bride, acknowledging his return squeeze. So far as she knew what she was doing, she meant to rub the yellow hairs between his knuckles and love him, which was touching, but which was dimmed by the fact that he had asked her a question about the keys of an organ and she had answered with something about cows.

He continued to examine her—there was nothing else to see but her top hair, her bangs, her eyes above the comb of flame along the lampwick; in the heat that now and then made the glass chimney tinkle and seem to swell. But he looked on with an uneasy wonder. How could eyes of which the balls seemed so intense not appear to see? And he thought of a picture in a church where his mother had dragged him daily for years in his boyhood, con-vinced that God would straighten out his flipper-like bad leg and even his toddering little hump, or, said she, being French and reasonable about bar-gains, God would make him some recompense; a bit of *lagniappe*, eh? But the picture? It took him a moment. He saw it between two round stone pil-lars, in a rift of incense that floated bluer, because the church was cold. It showed a saint kneeling on one knee in an improbable landscape of cliffs and rivers and peasants scything wheat. The saint was adoring Christ on the cross, just at hand; and the artist had made his gaze plain with straight lines at the wounds, lines of gold dashes so firm and literal that the dashes ended each with a raised gold blob. If Mother held you up, you made out the saint's fingernails and the wrinkles in his knuckles.

It was dizzying to think of it; sickening even to the stomach, like a look downward from a height; but Lola seemed to be worse off than the saint. She was seated at a point in her past. Her gold-dotted stare was trained upon two points of that—the shrieking of jays through the missing piece of a window, and her eager respectful longing for a cow with a tidy bag. But meanwhile she saw *him*, Otto. He was in this too, over the beaded glass ornaments around the top of the lamp chimney. His bulk was there opposite her and a part of her gold blobs had to go towards him.

He knew what that had taken out of her and he patted her hand, to let her know that he did know, hoping that that would help. It was contagious. They were both "thinking blue"—she about the harmless hairs on a cow's teat; he about a bunion on a saint's toe.

It was a taut moment; baffling because it seemed to bring them into a new and painful kind of union, and he sighed and felt the tension go out of him when Lola came awake; when she straightened up in her chair with a hand to her cheek, focussing her eye naturally toward a sound from without, from beyond the door to the other part of the house.

It was another song. Nothing like "When You and I Wair Young, Maggie." Something limber and bouncy. Something doing the latest steps, winking and bold and naughty. Its words went:

"Put your arms around me, honey!
Hold me tight!"

It practically added, *"Oh you kid!"* which, Otto knew, was the boys' present call to girls who made a point of passing the drug store in the town at night.

Whatever its merits, it served to shake Lola awake; to make her recognize the girls' singing, over their squeals, to the thud and trill of the pianola out in the big room; the long one with tables and chairs and pink, bead-fringed lamp shades.

"My Lord," she said (as if he and she had just been chatting), "I'm late. I've got to get out there!" And running into the bedroom to thrust a comb through her hair she disappeared . . . out there, away . . . with an absent-minded smile for Otto, leaving him, for the first time that he could remember, facing the cups, the bones and grease on the plates, the wadded napkins, all alone.

He leaned back in his chair. It amused him. He would get up and cope with this. He would run hot water and scrub and dry. She would be shamed and surprised, when she returned, but pleased, too, he hoped, to find all the dishes put away and the kitchen towels spread out to dry.

Meanwhile, since she was long in coming back, he leaned against the sink, warmed his hands in the suds and thought; mused and pondered. This strange behavior of Lola's just now at table, was it actually a single example and had it happened suddenly? He told himself that he was a simpleton. Nothing happens suddenly. A girder snaps, yes; an avalanche takes off down the mountain; a whole tree, rootwad and all, drops straight down from the edge of a cliff. But before that, there has to be slow rot, secret trickles, frosty swellings and meltings in the cracks of stone.

He had just not watched Lola, that was all. He had not, as women say, "noticed." Now that he felt about in the pan for the soap and stared at the taps, he realized that, for a long while, she had been changing; doing things, little things, but things out of character; cross over this trifle; miffed over that trifle; impatient, and given to lapses, treading on cats; standing between her chair and the fire, looking at her knitting but muttering where could it be; and even asking him, Otto, what there was for supper.

What was the cause of this? Had he mistaken her disposition in the first place? Was she concealing an illness? Was she addled, getting on in years? He was thinking in circles, making nothing of it; but, as summer came on, with hot light and a few knotty apples up under the leaves of the apple trees, two incidents occurred from which he thought he might get clues.

The first of them happened on a clear July morning. A Sunday. They sat at breakfast, passing things, spreading preserves on biscuits; basking in the sun that slanted in through the door; but, while they were enjoying the sound of church bells, they were disturbed by footsteps. Slow, dragging steps from behind the door at Lola's back. Whoever wore the shoes . . . and who could it be but one of the girls? . . . did not quite lift the heels, so that Lola lifted her nose as if she had smelled smoke. "Morning drinking!" she said. "We can't have that!"

But before she could turn about in her chair to rise, the door flew back. Effie—Effie-the-Wink, as Otto had known her—held the knob; clutched it lest she fall. She had grown fat, giving the impression (as she leaned forward) that she was about to let out one breast from the top of her pink dress. A strand of the rope-yellow hair that Otto remembered fell between her eyes; swayed between them while they looked down into Lola's when Lola, still seated, wheeled about. As matter-of-factly as a girl could, who had taken gin for breakfast, she said, "You stole my man."

She freed her hand from the knob, trying to point at Otto. "Old Crip over there," she said. "He come to me whenever he first come here. Now," she added and guffawed, an inch away from Lola's nose, "he's your little boy. You tuck him into bed every night and crawl right in after him, don't you?" And with an angry stare for Otto, whom she had just really made out, over the cream pitcher, she said, "All the time he was coming to me, all I was doing was just fattening a toad frog to feed a snake."

By now Lola had pushed back her chair and drawn up her skirts from her knees, suddenly resolute. She rose; faced Effie; and before Otto knew what she was about, she had reached behind her for the neck of a catsup bottle which she lifted up high and brought down on Effie's skull with a brief crack.

It was too late. By the time he had sprung to his feet, what he saw was Effie tilted backwards, rigid from the heel up, showing the white of her eyes, with overlapping scallops of catsup flooding down from her hair, like blood on the wooden heads of martyrs in the church back home.

He looked down into his plate. Lola had slammed the door. She made the motions of dusting her hands. "That settles that," she said, and sat down and re-addressed herself to her eggs. And he tried to eat too. It came hard. Violence between females he had never seen before. It made him go at his food gingerly. Who could say if a powder of glass from the bottle had not settled into the folds of his omelet, or caught upon the gravy over his grits?

*   *   *

The second incident had no brutality about it—certainly not on Lola's part (it was he who took a mallet and beat out the wall)—but, in its way, it was grimmer yet. An autumn sun was brightening the wings of grackles, gathered now into flocks, out in the lilac bushes and up in the apple trees . . . a warmish light smelling of walnut hulls and, with its floating blue, causing the roofs of the houses below the hill to seem to be farther down, and farther away. A Saturday. A day off with, so he felt in his bones, a promise of some time of dry weather.

He waited after breakfast until she had left. She went with that look of women who are going to sort out linen . . . There was the stump of her shoes on the second landing . . . There might be time.

Quickly, quickly, with his chisel and mallet, he chipped the outline of a window in the blank wall; scraped and tapped so well, lifting out the bricks when he could by hand, that before long he stood solemnly in the breeze and sunlight of the hole he had made along the side of the room. His lashes were whitened by mortar dust. He had to squint. But out beyond the gallery, the flock of grackles, gathering for autumn, had settled in one of the trees. To see out at all was a joy; to see so much life—the raised neck feathers and quivering wings almost outnumbering the leaves on the trees delighted him so that he did not hear Lola clear her throat behind him.

She had heard the noise. She had run down from upstairs to see. He had expected that, but he was not prepared for her frown beneath her bangs nor for her harsh question, "What do you think you're doing?"

Still he smiled. A few bricks had of course rolled on to the floor. Air moving in through the hole pushed sand across the table towards the cruets and sauce bottles. The stove, in the new light, looked both old and nude. He waited, giving her the time any woman would need to see that her kitchen had been wrecked.

At last he said, "I was making you a surprise."

"Ah," she said, and folded her arms.

"This," he went on, "is going to be a big bow window, with room on the ledge for cats and flower pots."

"Ah," she repeated. This time she stepped back to avoid a brick which gave way and fell from the sunny edge of the hole, but she did not unfold her arms.

It made him almost angry. He laid his mallet down on the table and said shortly, "You can already see out." She did not answer. When he turned back to her, having pointed to the birds, to the flues and gables of the houses on the slope below, her eyes were still expressionless, the lines of her mouth pinched. He saw that it was up to him to enlarge upon his plan.

"I am putting you in a window," he said carefully, as if she had been deaf or stupid. "I am putting you in a window so that you see out." Gesturing toward the part of the wall that was still soiled and blank, he thought of something. "After the life you've lived; after the life you've told me about," he said, "I thought it would raise your spirits to *see out*."

At least it made her break her pose. She took a backward step; raised one hand, showing him only the narrow side of it in an odd sort of liturgy-like motion that halted him, though what she pronounced was homely enough.

"Make yourself at home," she said. "Finish what you've started. I just do not," she added, with a look around at the bricks and his whitened lashes, "see what's to come of smarting up an old place like this now."

She was gone. She had turned the knob so that it made no echo amongst the sunny motes of the kitchen air. The space where she had stood was empty, and he looked down at his mallet, wilted as men are when their women make martyrs of themselves over a well-meant hole in a thing like an old pink wall.

"She just can't imagine how it's going to be"—he tried to tell himself that, but trailed off lamely. Seeing how things were going to be was what women were usually good at. Lola saw his window plainly. He was sure of that. But she was not only not pleased; she was in something like despair; it was all in her last word . . . "now" . . . before she'd got out the door.

"Why smarten up this old place now?" That was what she had said, and the dreadful part of it was that she'd placed no emphasis at all on the last word. It had simply floated out among the kitchen odors—the bite of ash, of wood smoke, and old grease—both much more sharp now that the outside air had got in.

*   *   *

She had staked him out (for what he was worth) as her own, on the day when she had struck Effie with the catsup bottle. He had got that well enough. It had amused him. But now what did "now" mean? Could she be saying that now she was going to leave this place it was no good his furbishing it up?

And he felt for a while like a dog watching his masters pack and buckle their grips, knowing that they were not going to take him with them—until presently a worse thought occurred. Did she mean to leave *and* take him with her? Remove him from this house and garden where, for the first time in his life, he felt no need to quail before anybody?

Where he could, so to speak, look the world in the eye?

His mind and his flesh refused that. And after dark he went to bed with a chill about his heart . . . . Perhaps she felt one too. She did not speak to him or touch him or even snore, from under the frills of her cap, until the room was already grey with dawn.

VI

HE WAS LATER TO THINK HOW, ONLY
recently, he'd been telling himself that nothing ever
happened fast. The avalanche, he had said, needed
weeks of rotting under it, before it let go and rolled
whole houses down the slope. Yet but then, for people inside the houses, the impression of suddenness
must be keen. So it was with him at any rate, on the
last night that he spent with Lola—with the old sane
and cheerful Lola whom he'd loved so much; to
whom he was still bottomlessly grateful.

When that night came, he'd have sworn that the
thing broke fast; that he was like a man knocked
about with the furniture in a room of a house tum-
bling over and over, breaking his bones, a house
rolled down by the avalanche.

He had had no inkling; no serious warning. For
days, weeks (or was it months?) she had been ir-
ritable; but why should he have seen, in that, more
than the effect of an old woman's aches and mum-
bles? She had also seemed to be absent-minded.
The pupils of her eyes had often appeared to swell
when he crossed their range, as if she had been asking herself how he had got into the landscape which
she "saw"; but, again, what of that? Young people
as well as old people—all people—commonly had
scenes of their supposed past to overlap those of
their supposed present.

No, but it had been sudden. No one could tell him
otherwise. And one thing had lead so innocently

into the next. The maple trees out beyond the apples at the edge of the yard had turned yellow-pink. Leaves, even in still air, twirled down from the apples. Lights, but companionable lights, were coming on in the houses down the hill. He and Lola had stepped out for a breath before supper. Walking over the turf between the gallery and the trees, both had declared that they felt a threat of frost through the soles of their shoes. They had pushed open the garden gate to go in after the last of the marigolds whose orange-colored blooms rose all the brighter over their rusty foliage in the dusk. In their haste they pulled up whole plants, since they were to die anyway, and snapped off the blooms.

Now they had come back. Now they stood at the foot of the steps leading to the kitchen; oddly, because their toes were cold in the grass; why did they not hurry up to the warm stove?

Perhaps it was because the weather was strange. They dallied a while to note that. A few high stars were out; high but big, with a winter twinkle. The garden would be nipped. And yet from down below, from the roofs and wispy chimneys, a mist was shaping up. It was spreading out over the withered grass on which they stood. And who had ever heard of fog and a hard frost on the same night?

It was then that the suddenness had seemed so sudden. He was watching the white haze, still shallow up where they were, but crawling toward their feet; thinking that it smelled of leaf mold and of how cosy the stove was about to be, when, shockingly, to his utter, honest male bewilderment, he felt her wheel him about by his arm to face her exactly, and heard her ask, "Listen! Will you take me away from here?"

He stood like an ox. She was there plainly enough before him; frowning out from under the brim of his old black felt hat. He got the tone of her words; felt them as he'd feel a woman's voice if she wanted help onto a train which had begun to move, whose cars were just at the point of going into speed. He even got the sense of her question—a bit, anyway; not in his mind as an idea however; rather, as he'd have got the squeal and dusty suction of the caboose of the train as it cleared the sheds.

He stood back from her on the cold grass and rubbed his nose, watching not her eyes but her load of flowers. Some of the heads drooped on broken stems, though she carried them like a bride. While she waited, he waited.

She waited, he suspected, because you had to give an ox time. He waited—he needed a silence—because what he had got of her drift struck him (like the real drops of mist on the yarn of her sweater) as the kind of drift you get in dreams . . . in moments when you breathe through your mouth onto a pillow and with glad smiles understand Persian or Swahili or Spanish; lingoes of which you know not a word by daylight. If, through all of this, he got even a blurred distortion of her question, of her command, "Take me away from here!", then he was at a greater loss than he was in sleep. Far more threatened and vulnerable.

Was he, pulling himself together out of these musings, to believe that she really meant to take him away from this nourishing house and garden?

Apparently so; there was *conclusion* in the angle of her head and in the lines about her eyes as she studied his face. Something proprietory. Something like a mother holding a switch to whip a boy. Something that made him feel, rather than know, in his weakening knees, that she was ready to do that preposterous thing; to bundle him in behind mules, into a wagon crowded with bedsteads and the pianola and basket-loads of shoes and odd plates and curtain rods. He already heard the wheels bobbing and grinding over the gravel of strange roads; he smelled the team's harness; he took in through his nostrils the panic of Abraham in the Testament, going out "not knowing whither."

And evidently, too, she was so set in her plan that she had made no room for resistance. She had gone through the argument, privately taking both parts herself, and won. What she wanted now was quick consent and she pinched him; plucked the flesh of his arm to wake him up and get his consent and stamped her foot and shook her bouquet when he wasted time; when he kept still, astonished, and blinked his blond bull's lashes at her.

To give her credit, though, she saw where she was (trying to get something new through a man's head) and she tried a tried female trick; she switched, or she seemed completely to switch, subjects. One way to get a ponderous beast through a gate.

"My Pa," she said, "was a hard man. He treated women like stock."

She buried her chin in the marigolds and arched her brows, giving him a smile to put him off the track, and went rapidly on.

"My Pa," she said, "he'd land his knuckles across a girl's nose with no more mind than he'd shoo off a mosquito."

Otto kept still. He smelled the sweat and lathering of mule harness more keenly than the bruised marigold leaves. Furthermore he sensed that Lola was about to say something strange, which she did.

"Now that I've got this far along in life," she continued, raising her voice, "I see that Pa was not always wrong. He was trying to save a girl's soul."

Her addition . . . "That's what he was meaning to do" . . . was spoiled by a pricking trill from the pianola in the main body of the house. It gurgled, muted by the closed windows; but the girls, shifting their garters and combing one another's head, brought its message out through the misty panes. "Oh, you beautiful doll!" they shrilled, "you great big beautiful doll!"

Even Lola looked up. Otto had a second to think.

When she had hit Effie over the head with the bottle, she had marked him off for hers. Nobody else's. Now she wanted to take him away to a woodsy spot where the claim could not be contested. So. That much was clear. What stayed murky was her sudden conversion to her daddy's jay-bird religion. Or was it sudden? Hadn't Otto just been the fellow assuring himself that nothing happened fast? Could it be that, in Lola's warm breasty torso, the throb had been there all the time; the chapped fingers, the nasal hymns? Was he that stupid? It must be true.

She was saying how Pa would claim it was bringing down the Wrath; it was calling for Flame to live under the roof of a house like this. And she exclaimed again, as if the fire had already been eating at her hair, "Get me out of here! Take me away from here!"

Otto was trembling too hard to answer. He had always thought of religion as of pomp, of gold cherubs puffing into horns, of organ bursts . . . or, if it struck him personally, as something lulling, something officially reassuring. Like the mayor with his sash. And now here was this woman screaming at him with her mouth open, close to his face, like a snake's.

He was also distracted by, of all people on earth, the girls. It was their jolly hour, their giggling time of shaking out combs and feeling for garters just before the gentlemen arrived, when a kind of suppressed hysteria kindled among them. Their forms in loose gowns were going and coming behind the panes of the "big room." To the pounding and trill of the pianola, which Otto felt even out on the earth beneath his shoes, they were singing.

"Oh, you beautiful doll, you great big beautiful doll!
I'd like to hug you but I'm 'fraid you'd break!"

So it went. A mindless noise like that of schoolgirls excited by one another's shrieks; switching their skirts in unison and getting out one of the songs of their school. They came and went and "did" one another's heads. A chimney above them smoked out of the roof into the wind.

Lola was still waiting with her eyebrows up and her mouth open. Waiting for an answer. Apparently she granted that it would take time—how much time she did not know—nor did he. He was too like a fellow who has trod upon a live electric wire. Not a main one that would sizzle him to death, but one that could make his hair stand up and rattle his molars.

There was the thump and trill of the piano and the pull of the girls' rhythmic hum, both of them playing hard against Lola's singed cry for safety from the Flame. It was enough to try thinking against that. But there was worse. Why did Lola stand there before him with her mouth open—why didn't she close it? Perhaps it was an idiotically small detail, but it roused a kind of dread in him. Also, why had she crushed his old hat so that her head looked flat? And why, especially, did she stare at him as if she had been looking through some kind of murky glass?

Above all, could she have possibly forgot that she had been his angelic agent; his means of crawling under this oatmeal box, this humped old house full of dime perfume, with yellow spots on the sheets, but where he had been transformed? Where the imbalance of his back, with its wag and twitch, had been struck off the score? Where he was gratefully taken as a creature with chest hair and strong arms, with such thick calves? Where he had been so welcomed when he entered the warm air of the kitchen with a center cut of pork loin under his arm? Had she forgot the waxy crackle of the butcher's paper? the cut string? the lovely pink pig flesh that would guard a girl's gut against hunger? He, a man, had brought it to her, under the sleeve of his coat? A man who limped but had the pork?

Of course you never knew what a male or a female would do when fire went over the small hairs of the forearm and the mouth stayed open with pain. It behooved you to smother your own will, to beat down your own interest; to steel yourself to brush the fire away from someone else's burned-off nose.

He had to puzzle it out fast; to think of Lola, quick. He wanted at least to make some sign; to hold out his hands to her from where he stood in the smoke of the girls' chimney; even to hand her up, if he had to, onto the seat behind the mules, before the load of jiggling baskets covered by quilts and old house-dresses. If she would only stop showing her teeth under the crushed hat! If she would only do anything to take his mind, and his nostrils, off the smoke!

It was a rich smoke; full of unconsumed particles; and it flattened out straight away when it came from the flue in the wind, parting like two ribbons, to get by him. It smelled of a good nourished braise from down below somewhere, in the girls' big room. In a falling off of the wind it wreathed around and around him with a scorched whiff of roasted chestnut shells, a flutter of tent flaps, a lion's roar. The chipped saints of a church front, one missing an ear, another lacking half of his beard, these had seen centuries of such fairs. Saint Vaast's, Otto thought he remembered the church was. The fire was a bonfire lighted on the cobbles of the *parvis*. It sent its chestnut-scented smoke past the flaking cheeks of the saints; under scalloped tent flaps; into booths where you threw balls; past the smell of lion's staling and around Otto's legs. He was breathless. He had just outrun a gaggle of kids who thought, because of his hump, that he was part of the show. Why did he not have a purple nose? Where were the white and red diamonds beneath his eyes? They had yelled such things as that and tried to hug his leg.

Now he stood panting in the smoke that thinned out around the church spire; warmed his hands over the coals; and gazed about at the exhibitions. Two painted wagons (both blue, with roses and daisies) were drawn up close by—one with a drowsy lion, tired after its roar; another, glassed in, with a pythoness that caught his attention.

He had never seen so gross a serpent. She would have been as tall as a woman had she stood erect. This was not likely. She, too, was tired; and, though she might have been burning furiously within, she lay limp in a kind of braided ring, as if to move at all were the last thing she meant to do in this damned world. Only a spreading pattern of skin, flattened against her smudgy glass, now and then let on that she had breath . . . . But suddenly the hairs on Otto's neck turned stiff. She had changed her mind. Slow and fat, using her face as a pusher, she thrust off of her coil far enough to lift two feet of her neck; to glare at Otto out of her level head and to give him a red and bare-fanged hiss.

He took it personally. What she thought he had done to her? Why, in that brief glance of hate and contempt, in that show of pinkish sacs and teeth, did she think for a moment that *he* had helped put her into that bad air behind the muddied pane? Why, if he could, he'd have brought her a rat or a pig's leg. He actually wanted to tap upon her glass and tell her some such thing; to say that, if she promised not to swallow him when he lowered her window, she should have flesh. But she had written him off. He was like the rest. He had not been worth her saliva. Her hiss has become a yawn. She had placed her chin back on the top of her mounded circle and gone to sleep, perhaps to dream of free downward loops from branches of trees nameless to him, with a lion cub in her belly. Did she have at least that? The dream and the power to shut off, for herself, the stamp and snort of the calliope and the chant of the chestnut vendor? Could she, at need, as he could, seal off a moment of Time when she was both captive and loose?

*   *   *

The smoke felt warm while his feet felt frost. Lola had lost her patience. She had dug her nails into his arm. Her face was at his. Her breath smelt milky. His whole sense of her presence—her hat, her nose, her bosom, her stomach under her house-dress,—was so strangely close and so caused him to feel that he'd missed the last step of a stair, but, miraculously, not broken his glasses, that he trembled, and when she whispered, "One last time. Get this. Will you take me away from here?", he said: "No."

His lips said it. He'd have sworn that somebody or something else had done it. He had not meant to be misunderstanding and cruel, much less abrupt. The word had come out of him like a grunt.

And it had been a wonder that he'd been able to

make even so brief a sound as that. He felt stupid; too clogged and choked up to talk; too baffled by a set of pressing but counterwise impressions to draw out of himself one clear, sensible statement. There was the smoke and the girls' jolly rocking song. It confused him that the smoke smelled of hickory logs, not of chestnut shells. There was the unnatural fog. It mixed him up that it should *be* at all, on a night when his toes were cold; that it should plait itself around his and Lola's knees, while she still stood, giving him one last long chance; that it should float up, thinning itself out below her eyes which he suddenly—this particularly threw him off—suddenly saw were not blue and had not been blue all the time. They were thistle-colored. A kind of purple with grey tones.

The fact that this should matter he took as a sign that he was living through a time of the sort men get into when they fall, shot, with a rush of blood from between two ribs, or at any rate when they slip off a ladder (holding a gallon of paint) and lie in the grass with the wind knocked out of them, idiotically fixing their gaze on an ant; a large black ant walking over a dandelion.

What good did it do him to know the color of Lola's eyes now? When his silence made her spring, spring up the stairs as if she'd been touched in her tender parts by something intolerable from below— a spark-shedding wire; by a thought that raised blisters? When all he saw of her was her back on the steps; her flat hat, her nape, her sloping shoulders and a good display of old lady's stocking tops?

She had pulled up her dress, the better to make

speed; the better to get away from him and all his kind. Still, as he'd have watched the black ant, he saw that she crooked her legs apart as women of a certain number of winters do . . . . Even at such a moment, with fog in his nose, he watched her legs . . . . That, like a second large ant, impressed him; and he saw them as frowsy and full-blown about the garters, but, below that, still well-formed, and, above all, amazingly strong.

No wonder then that, when she had cleared the steps, she was able to do what she did in the thin mist that had reached the gallery. Through it he saw her put her arms akimbo and stretch out her knees beneath her skirt, to make a kind of heathen figure-X of herself, such as he'd seen in books on Guatemala; a thing still clear on stone under lichen, but nothing you could bow your Christian head to. Besides, you had no time. You had to dodge. She spat at you. She said, "God damn all men," devoutly, as if that came right after "and fill all hands with plenteousness," and you felt as if your pants had dropped off during a deep-felt genuflection; because the eyes of the girls were upon you.

All of them, all of them that could find room to rub spots in the panes of the "big room" were not missing a stroke. Like hens that bloody one anothers' combs, they had "got" madam's humiliation and mad distress and it served the old dame right and they blew upon the holes they'd made to make them wider; and Otto felt, at the sight of their happy nods, what he'd have called in French "*death in his soul*." Mildew; green growth on bones, and not so much from Lola, who spun his flat hat at him like a quoit and went into the kitchen, as from the girls behind the rubbed spots. There he saw skulls with wigs; eye holes; nose holes; Y-shaped mouths—all like the candied heads given to children to suck, on All Saints' Night, in distant lands.

For a little he'd have felt about in the fog for the post of the stair and rested his head on it. Give him one little push and he'd have let out a sob. "Be it all according to Thy will," he'd have said. And he'd have added as, in effect, he found himself doing— while he picked up Lola's hat—in the language of his wide-bottomed father, *du lieber allmächtiger Gott*!

About the author

Ward Dorrance, a native of Missouri and a graduate of the University of Missouri, is Professor Emeritus of English at Georgetown University, Washington, D.C. A one-time Guggenheim fellow, he is the author of the novels, *The Party at Mrs. Purefoy's* (Delacorte) and *The Sundowners* (Scribner's), co-author of *The White Hound* (Missouri), and of a number of short stories and scholarly works.